THE GOBLIN
AEROPLANE

Enid Blyton's

THE GOBLIN
AEROPLANE
and other stories

RED FOX

A Red Fox Book
Published by Arrow Books Limited
20 Vauxhall Bridge Road, London SW1V 2SA

An imprint of the Random Century Group

London Melbourne Sydney Auckland
Johannesburg and agencies throughout the world

First published by Pitkin, London 1949 and 1951
Red Fox edition 1990

Phototypeset in Plantin 12/14 pt by
Input Typesetting Ltd, London
Made and printed in Great Britain by
Courier International Ltd, Tiptree, Essex

ISBN 0 09 973590 3

Contents

The
Goblin Aeroplane

'IT's such a lovely day you can take your lesson books on to the hillside, if you like,' said Mummy one morning to Jill and Robert.

So out they went.

'What have you got to do?' Robert asked Jill.

'I've got to learn how to spell six words,' said Jill. 'They're rather hard. Here they are: mushroom, toadstool, honey, dewdrop, magic and enchantment. Don't you think they are hard, Robert?'

'Yes,' said Robert. 'I'm sure I don't know how to spell them. I've got to learn my seven times table.'

'I'm only up to five times,' said Jill. 'Ooh, isn't it lovely out on the hillside, Robert!'

The two children sat down and opened their books – but it was hard to work. First a lovely peacock butterfly flew by. Then a tiny copper beetle with a shining back ran over Jill's book. Then a robin came and sat so near to them that they hardly dared to move in case he was frightened away.

'I say, Jill!' said Robert at last. 'How much work have you done?'

'None!' said Jill. 'Have you learnt your table, Robert?'

'Only as far as seven times two,' answered Robert. 'It's a pity to have to do homework when the sun is shining so brightly and we'd like to play.'

'Well, let's not do it,' said Jill. 'No one will know, because we can take our books to bed with us tonight, and after Mummy has gone we can get them out and learn our words and our tables then!'

'Oh, no, Jill!' said Robert, shocked. 'Mummy trusted us to do our lessons here, and we must. It would be mean to play when she sent us out here for a treat.'

'All right,' said Jill. 'It would be mean – so let's get on quickly and finish them, Robert.'

The two children turned their backs on one another, put their fingers in their ears and began to learn their spelling and table. They didn't look up once even when the robin flew down at their feet. They meant to do their lessons really properly.

Soon Jill sat up.

'I've finished, Robert!' she said. 'Hear my spelling, will you?'

'Yes, if you'll hear my seven times table,' said Robert. They passed each other their books, and Jill was just beginning to spell 'Mushroom' when a very strange thing happened.

They saw a tiny speck in the sky, which rapidly grew larger. It was bright red and yellow.

'It's an aeroplane, Jill!' said Robert. 'But what a funny one!'

It certainly was odd, for instead of having flat wings like an ordinary aeroplane, it had curved

wings like a bird, and it flapped these slowly up and down as it flew.

'It's coming down!' said Jill, in excitement. 'Ooh, look, Robert, it's coming down quite near us!'

Sure enough the strange aeroplane flew swiftly towards them, flapping its odd red and yellow wings. From the cockpit a funny little man peeped out. He waved his hand to them.

The aeroplane suddenly dipped downwards, and with a whirr of wings that sounded rather like a giant bee buzzing, it landed on the hillside near the excited children. They ran up to it in astonishment.

'What a tiny aeroplane!' cried Robert. 'I've never seen one like that before!'

'It's a goblin aeroplane!' said the pilot inside, peeping at them and grinning widely. 'It belongs to me.'

'Are you a goblin then?' asked Jill, in surprise.

'Of course,' said the strange pilot, and he jumped out of his 'plane. Then the children saw that he really was a goblin. His ears were pointed and stuck out above his cap. His body was round and fat, and his feet were as pointed as his ears.

'I've come to ask if you can tell me where Greenfield Farm is,' he said.

'Oh yes,' said Robert. 'It's over that field, then through a path in the wood, then over a stile, then down by the stream, then over the little hill, then–'

'Goodness!' cried the goblin, 'I shall never find it in my aeroplane! Can't you tell me how to get to it from the air?'

'I might, if I were in your aeroplane with you,' said Robert, doubtfully. 'I think I should know what the farm looks like, but I couldn't quite tell you now how to go. You see, I've never been in an aeroplane.'

'Well come for a ride in mine,' said the goblin, grinning. 'You and your sister can both come, and as soon as you show me Greenfield Farm and I land there, you can hop out and run home again.'

'Ooh!' shouted both children in excitement, and they danced up and down in glee. 'Do you really mean it?'

'Of course,' said the goblin. 'Come on, hop in.'

So they climbed into the aeroplane, and the goblin climbed in too. Jill and Robert looked to see how he flew it. It was a very strange aeroplane, there was no doubt of that. In front of the goblin's seat were dozens of little buttons, each with something printed on. One had 'Down' on, one had 'Up', and another had 'Sideways'. Still another had 'Home' on, and a fifth had 'Fast', and a sixth one 'Slow'. There were many more besides.

The goblin pressed the button marked 'Up' and the aeroplane began to flap its strange wings. It rose from the ground, and the children clutched the sides in excitement, for it was a very odd feeling to be in something that flapped its wings and flew into the air.

'There's the farm!' cried Robert, and he pointed to a pretty farm house over to the east. At once the goblin pressed a button marked 'East', and the aeroplane flapped its way to the right. Soon it was over the farm, but to the children's great surprise it didn't land, but flew straight on.

'Aren't you going to land?' asked Jill. 'You've passed right over the farm.'

'Ha ha!' laughed the goblin, and it was such a nasty laugh that the children looked at him in surprise.

'Why don't you land?' asked Robert. 'I don't want to go too far, you know, because of getting home again.'

'You're going to come with me!' said the

goblin. 'You didn't suppose I really wanted to go to the farm, did you? Why that was only a trick to get you both into my aeroplane!'

The children sat silent for a minute, they were so surprised. Jill felt frightened.

'What do you want us for?' asked Robert at last.

'To sell to Big-One the giant,' said the goblin. 'He's lonely in his castle and he wants two children to talk to.'

'But, good gracious, you can't do a thing like that!' cried Robert, in a rage. 'Take us back home at once, or I'll make you very sorry for yourself!'

The goblin smiled a wide smile, and said nothing. Robert wondered what to do. He did not dare to hit the goblin, for he was afraid that the aeroplane might fall. So he just sat there frowning, holding Jill's hand tightly, for he saw that she was frightened.

After about twenty minutes Robert looked over the side of the aeroplane. Far below was a strange-looking country with palaces gleaming on hills, and castles towering high.

'It must be Fairyland,' whispered Jill when Robert pointed it out to her. 'Oh, Robert, this

is a great adventure, even if that old goblin is
taking us to a giant!'

Just then the aeroplane plunged downwards,
for the goblin had pressed the button marked
'Down'. It flew to a great castle standing on a
mountain top, and landed on one of the towers.
The goblin leapt out and ran to a staircase
leading down from the roof.

'Hey, Big-One!' he called. 'Here are two
children for you! Where's that sack of gold you
promised me?'

Robert and Jill heard great footsteps coming
up the stairs, and a giant's head peeped out on
to the roof. He had a huge shock of hair, a
turned-up nose, a wide mouth and very nice
blue eyes as big as dinner plates. The children
liked the look of him much better than they
liked the goblin.

'So these are the children,' said the giant, in a
loud booming voice. 'Well, they look all right,
goblin. You can have your sack of gold tonight.
I haven't any by me at the moment. Come for it
at six o'clock.'

'All right,' said the goblin, and he went back
to the aeroplane.

'Climb out,' he ordered, and Robert and Jill
climbed down from the cockpit, feeling very

14

strange. The goblin leapt into his seat, pressed the button marked 'Up' and disappeared into the sky, shouting that he would be back that night at six o'clock for his sack of gold without fail.

The giant looked at the two children.

'Will you come down into my kitchen?' he said, in a kind voice. 'I am sure you want something to eat and drink after your ride.'

Robert and Jill felt glad to hear him speak so politely. He couldn't be very fierce, they thought. They followed him down the enormous stairs and came to a vast kitchen where a huge kettle boiled loudly on a great fire.

'Sit down,' said Big-One, and he pointed to two chairs. But neither Robert nor Jill could climb on to the seats, for they were so high up. So the giant gently lifted them up, and then took the boiling kettle from the stove.

He made some cocoa in three great china cups, and set out three enormous plates, on each of which he had placed a very large slice of currant cake.

'Please join me in a little lunch,' he said. 'It is really very kind of you to take pity on me and come to live with me. I didn't think any children would be willing to come here, you know.'

'Why, we weren't willing!' said Robert, in astonishment. 'The goblin got us here by a trick. We didn't want to come here at all!'

'What!' cried the giant, upsetting his cocoa in his surprise. 'Do you mean to say that nasty little goblin brought you here against your will?'

'Yes,' said Robert, and he told Big-One all about the morning's happenings.

Jill listened and nodded her head, eating her currant cake, which was really most delicious.

The giant was terribly upset when he heard about the trick that the goblin had played on the children.

'I don't know what to do!' he said, and two big tears stood in his saucer-eyes. 'I wouldn't have had such a thing happen for the world! Now, however can I get you back again? And oh, dear me, that nasty goblin will be coming for his sack of gold too, and I haven't any. You see, I thought you'd be able to help me with my spells, for children are very clever, much cleverer than stupid giants like me. I thought I'd get you to help me with a gold-spell, and make some gold before the evening.'

'Well, we don't mind helping you a bit,' said Robert, who liked the big giant very much.

'Don't cry. You've splashed a tear into your cocoa, and it will make it taste salty.'

'Will you really help me!' cried Big-One. 'Oh, you good, kind children! Well, I'll just clear away these things and then we'll set about making a gold-spell.'

He put the cups and plates into a huge sink and washed them up. Then he took the children into a big bare room with many chalk circles drawn on the floor. A big pot hung over a fire that burnt with strange green flames.

'Now first of all I've got to write six words in the biggest of these chalk circles,' he said. 'But, oh dear me, I don't know how to spell them! Still, children are very clever, so I do hope you'll be able to help me. Can either of you spell Mushroom?'

'I can!' cried Jill, excitedly. 'I learnt it this very morning! M-U-S-H-R-O-O-M!'

The giant carefully wrote it down in the circle as Jill spelt it. Then he looked up at her.

'Now could you spell Magic?' he asked.

'Yes!' said Jill, 'M-A-G-I-C! That was one of the words I had to learn this morning, too!'

Well, would you believe it, all the words that the giant needed for his spells were the very ones Jill had to learn! Wasn't it a good thing she

17

had done them so well? The last one the giant wanted was Enchantment.

'That's the hardest one,' said Jill, and she frowned. 'Oh, I do hope I remember it properly. Let me see – E-N–'

'Where's your spelling book, Jill?' asked Robert, terribly afraid that Jill might spell the word wrong after all. 'You could look it up before you spell it.'

'We left both our books on the hillside!' said Jill. 'No, I must try and spell it out of my head. Let me think for a minute – yes, I think I've got it. E-N-C-H-A-N-T-M-E-N-T!'

Big-One wrote it carefully down. Then he drew a toadstool and a mushroom right in the very middle of the circle, put a spot of honey on each, and shook a dewdrop from a piece of grass on to the honey.

'That's all ready for the spell now!' he said. 'What a good thing you knew how to spell Mushroom, Toadstool, Honey, Dewdrop, Magic and Enchantment, Jill. But oh, dear me – the next thing we have to do is very hard!'

'What's that?' asked Robert.

'Well, two of us have to dance round the circle holding hands,' said the giant, 'whilst one stands in the middle chanting the seven times table. But I don't know the seven times table. I only know twice times.'

'I don't know it either,' said Jill.

'But I do!' cried Robert. 'I learnt it this very morning. I can say it! I'll be the one to stand in the middle.'

'Oh, good!' said Big-One, and he rubbed his great hands together in delight. 'Now listen – Jill and I will dance round together, and you must stand still in the middle saying your seven times table at the top of your voice. At the end of it I have to say twelve very magic words, and then, if we've done the spell right, a sack of gold appears right in the middle of the circle!'

'Come on, let's do it!' cried Jill. 'Are you sure you know all your seven times perfectly, Robert? It might spoil the spell if you got something wrong.'

'I'm not quite sure of seven times twelve,' said Robert. 'I think it's eighty-four, but just wait a minute and I'll work it out to make sure.'

He took a piece of the giant's chalk and wrote the figure 12 seven times on the floor. Then he added them up, and sure enough, it made eighty-four, so he was quite right.

Then they started the spell. Jill and the giant danced round the circle, and Robert stood in the middle saying his seven times table at the top of his voice. When he had finished the giant shouted out a string of curious magic words, and all the words he had written inside the ring suddenly vanished!

Then crash! A great sack suddenly appeared in the middle of the circle and knocked Robert down. He was up in a minute, and peeped into the mouth of the sack.

'Yes, the spell has worked!' he cried. 'It's full of gold! Ooh, what powerful magic! And what a mercy I knew my seven times table properly!'

The giant was so pleased. He could hardly thank Robert and Jill enough.

'You don't know how grateful I am to you,' he said. 'I can pay that horrid goblin now, though I don't think he deserves a penny, because he brought you here by a trick. But the next thing is – how am I going to get you home again?'

'I don't know,' said Robert. 'Could you use magic, do you think?'

'No,' said Big-One. 'I don't know any that would take you home. Wait a minute – let me think.'

He sat down on a stool and frowned for five

minutes. Then he jumped up and clapped his hands so loudly that it quite frightened Jill.

'I've a fine plan!' he said. 'The goblin will come in his aeroplane tonight at six o'clock. Now listen – I'll hide you behind a chimney pot on the roof of the castle. When the goblin arrives I'll call him downstairs to the cellar to fetch his gold. As soon as he's gone down the stairs you must pop out, jump into the aeroplane and fly home!'

'But we don't know how to fly a goblin aeroplane!' said Robert.

'Oh, it's quite easy,' said Big-One. 'Didn't you see all those buttons? Well, you just press the one that says 'Up' and then the one that says 'Home', and then the one that says 'Down' when you see your home, and there you are!'

'Well, I think I could do that,' said Robert. 'Anyway, I'll try. But what shall we do till six o'clock?'

'Perhaps you'd like to come out with me in my yellow motor-car and see the sights of Fairyland?' said the giant.

'Ooh, yes!' cried the children. So the giant took them out to his great motor-car, and they climbed into it. What a time they had! They saw elves and fairies, brownies and gnomes, pixies and witches, and all kinds of strange little folk. They went into glittering palaces, they had dinner with a wizard and tea with a brownie, so you can guess what a glorious day they had. They were sorry when half-past five came, and the giant took them back to his castle.

He took them up to the roof and showed them a chimney to hide behind. Then he shook hands with both of them, and thanked them very much for all their help.

'Thank you for the lovely day you've given us,' said the children. 'We only wish we could stay longer, but our mother would be worried if we did.'

'Sh! Here comes the goblin!' said Big-One, suddenly. He ran down the stairs, and the children were left alone behind their chimney. They heard a whirring sound, and saw the red and yellow aeroplane flying down, its strange wings flapping as it came.

The goblin landed neatly on the roof and ran to the stairs.

'Where's my sack of gold, Big-One?' he cried.

'Come down and fetch it!' came the giant's booming voice. 'It's in my cellar.'

The goblin raced down the stairs. As soon as he was gone Robert and Jill ran to the aeroplane and climbed into it. Robert pressed the button marked 'Up', and the aeroplane at once rose upwards. Then he pressed the button marked 'Home', and the machine turned round in the air and flew steadily towards the setting sun.

Jill looked back and saw the goblin standing on the roof of the castle, shouting wildly. The giant stood beside him, laughing. They could hear his great 'Ho-ho-ho' for a long way.

The aeroplane flew steadily onwards. Suddenly Jill gave a cry and pointed downwards.

'There's our house, Robert!' she cried. 'Press the 'Down' button quickly!'

Robert pressed it. The aeroplane swooped down and landed on the hillside where the children had sat learning their lessons that morning. Robert and Jill jumped out, picked up their books which were still where they had left them, and raced home.

'Why, my dears, wherever have you been?' cried their mother. 'I have been so worried about you!'

'Oh Mummy, we've had such an adventure!' cried Robert. 'We've been up in a goblin aeroplane!' and he told her all that happened.

Their mother was so astonished that she simply couldn't say a word.

'Come and see the aeroplane,' said Robert. 'It's out on the hillside.'

They all three ran to the hill – but just as they got there they heard a whirring sound and Robert pointed up in the air.

'There it goes!' he cried. 'I expect it's gone back to the goblin. Oh, Mummy, I wish you'd seen all the buttons inside, and had come for a ride with us.'

'But that's not an aeroplane,' said their mother. 'It's only a very big bird. I can see its wings flapping.'

'No, really, it's the goblin aeroplane,' said Jill. But I don't think their mother believed it.

'Anyhow, my dears,' she said, as they all went home again. 'What a very good thing it was that you were good and learnt your lessons properly this morning – else you might have had to stay with that giant!'

And it was a good thing, wasn't it?

The
Little Pink Pig

THERE was once a little pink pig who lived
with his mother and nine other piglets in a
comfortable sty. His name was Curly because
he had such a twisty tail, and he was a very
plump little fellow indeed.

But he was not as good as the others. He was
always grumbling because he couldn't go into
the fields with the cows, and couldn't go on the
pond with the ducks.

'Be content,' said his mother. 'You are a little
pig, not a cow or a duck. You should be happy
to live at peace in a nice comfortable sty.'

'Pigs are silly creatures!' said the little pig
rudely. 'They do nothing but grunt! I wish I
wasn't a pig! I have a good mind to run away
and be something else!'

'Don't be foolish!' said his mother, and she
gave him a push with her snout. 'Lie down by
me and go to sleep in the nice warm sun.'

But the little pig wouldn't. He grunted crossly

and ran to the other side of the sty. The gate was there and the little pig looked underneath the lowest bar. The world seemed very exciting outside. There was Gobble the turkey making a tremendous noise. There was Dobbin the horse stamping with his foot. There was Rover the dog barking madly.

'Why was I born a little pink pig?' sighed Curly. 'If only I could live with Rover or Gobble or with the white ducks on the pond!'

He pushed his little snout farther under the gate and began to push himself through. Suddenly he slipped right underneath, and there he was in the farmyard!

'Ho!' said the little pink pig to himself. 'This is fine! This is the world! Now I shall no longer be a little pink pig, but I shall be a turkey or a dog or a horse. I will go to Dobbin and ask him to teach me to be a horse.'

So he trotted over to Dobbin, who was most surprised to see Curly in the farmyard.

'Please, said Curly, 'I want to be a horse. Pigs are silly creatures. Tell me what I must do to be a horse.'

Dobbin thought that the little pink pig was very foolish.

'You must neigh like this!' he said, and he

put his head down and neighed loudly in Curly's ear. The little pig fell over with fright.

'Then you must kick like this!' said Dobbin, and he kicked out with his hind legs, sending the little pink pig right up into the air. Curly came down with a splash in the pond. How frightened he was!

'Quack!' said the ducks swimming round. 'Quack!'

'Oh, I won't be a horse!' said Curly. 'They are horrid creatures. I will be a duck!'

So he spoke to the surprised ducks round him.

'Please,' he said, 'I want to be a duck. Pigs are silly creatures. Tell me what I must do to be a duck.'

The ducks thought that the little pink pig was very foolish.

'You must quack like this,' they said, and they all crowded round him, quacking so loudly that he was nearly deafened.

'Then you must peck like this!' they said, and began pecking him all over his body till he grunted in terror and ran out of the water as fast as ever he could.

'Oh, I won't be a duck!' cried Curly in a rage. 'They are horrid creatures. I will be a dog.'

So he went to where old Rover the yard-dog lay half in and half out of his kennel.

'Please,' he said. 'I want to be a dog. Pigs are silly creatures. Tell me what I must do to be a dog.'

Rover thought that the little pink pig was very foolish.

'You must bark like this!' he said, and made such a loud noise in Curly's ear that the pig turned pale with fright.

'Then you must bite like this!' said the dog, and bit Curly's tail very hard indeed. The little

pig squeaked loudly and ran away in a great hurry.

'Oh, I won't be a dog!' he cried in a temper. 'Dogs are horrid creatures. I will be a farmer!'

He saw Mr Straws the Farmer in the distance, and ran up to him. He thought it would be very grand to be a man and own everything on the farm.

'Please,' he said, 'I want to be a farmer. Pigs are silly creatures. Tell me what I must do to be a farmer.'

Mr Straws thought that the little pink pig was very foolish.

'You must shout like this!' he said, and he shouted at Curly so loudly that the pig ran away.

'Then you must punish naughty pigs like this!' said the farmer, and he began to spank Curly with his big stick. The little pig ran faster and came at last to his sty. He squeezed under the lowest bar and fled to his mother.

His mother grunted softly. All the other piglets squeaked happily, and rooted about in the straw. The sun shone warmly. The sty looked very comfortable and happy.

The little pink pig looked about him, and grunted.

'Oh, I have been very foolish,' he sighed.

'How lovely it is to hear grunts instead of barks and quacks! How comfortable my sty is! What sweet creatures pigs are! How glad I am to be a piglet and not a horrid horse, or dog or duck!'

And the little pink pig settled down to be a good pig, and was happy ever afterwards.

The Runaway Toys

DIANE and David had more toys than any other children in the town. Their playroom was full of dolls, teddy-bears, a toy clown, soldiers, Noah's arks, balls, trains and bricks. You would think they were happy, contented children with such a lovely lot of playthings, but they weren't.

They were spoilt, disagreeable children, very unkind to their dolls and teddies, and not a bit generous with all their toys. Diane would rather break a doll than give it away, and David would stamp on his soldiers rather than give a boxful to some child who had no toys at all.

So you can guess what kind of children they were. Their toys hated them, and trembled whenever Diane and David came into the playroom.

'I'm afraid Diane will pull off my arm,' said a pretty doll.

'I'm afraid David will tear off my nose,' whispered the clown.

'Diane might break us all,' groaned the Noah's ark animals.

'And David will certainly overwind me and break my spring,' said the clockwork train, with a sigh.

Now one evening, half an hour before bedtime, Diane and David had a quarrel. Diane wanted to play with David's soldiers, and he wouldn't let her. So she snatched a boxful away from him, and shouted that she was going to have them.

'If you take my soldiers, I'll take your dolls!' said Tom in a rage, and he pounced on a baby doll and a pretty talking doll.

Then what a fight there was! Diane smacked David and David punched Diane and pulled her hair. The soldiers were trodden on and broken, the two dolls lay trembling on their faces, one with its arm broken and the other with its dress torn to rags. David kicked the clown into a corner and Diane trod heavily on a teddy-bear, who growled angrily.

Soon their mother came running into the room wondering what the noise was.

'You naughty children!' she cried. 'You shall

both go to bed at once! Just look at your poor toys!'

The children had to go to bed there and then, and the toys were left scattered all over the floor. There they lay until the clock struck twelve.

As soon as the last stroke died away, the clown sat up and looked round.

'Well, toys!' he said, in a mournful voice, 'what a dreadful evening this has been!'

The dolls sat up and so did the teddy-bear. The baby doll cried because her arm was broken, and the clown tied it up gently for her.

'I do think Diane and David are just the worst children in the world!' said the talking doll, angrily, looking at her torn frock. 'I wish we didn't belong to them!'

'So do I!' said Mr Noah, climbing out of the ark, and looking sadly at some of his broken animals on the floor.

'Well, why should we stop with them!' said the captain of the soldiers. 'Here's half my men wounded by those unkind children! I declare I won't stay with them a day longer!'

'Ooh!' said all the toys in wonder. 'But how can we go away? We've nowhere to go to!'

'We needn't bother about where to go,' said Mr Noah, excitedly. 'The first thing is to go!'

'I'll take you!' said the clockwork train importantly. 'I think there's enough room in my carriages for most of you, only you'll have to take the roofs off, because you're too big, most of you, to get in through the doors.'

What an excitement there was in the playroom. Six dolls, two teddy-bears, twenty-two soldiers, all Mr Noah's family and animals, and a woolly sheep managed to get into the train, after Mr Noah had slid the roofs off all the carriages. It was a dreadful squeeze, but nobody minded.

Then the clown wound up the train and jumped into the cab to drive it. Off they went over the playroom floor, and out through the door. Down the passage they ran, the wheels making no noise at all on the carpet. The side-door swung open to let them through, and the train ran into the garden, puffing and panting with its load of happy toys.

Down the road it ran, passing a most astonished policeman, who could hardly believe his eyes. Then it turned down a lane, and came to a stop. The clown got out and wound the train up again and once more it started off. It ran for a very long way, and at last said that it was really getting very tired, and what about finding somewhere to stop for the night?

'There's a cottage near by,' said the clown. 'Let's go and see if any children are there, and if they look nice or not.'

So off went the train again and stopped just outside the cottage. The clown and the teddy-bears climbed up on the window sill and looked in. It was a very poor cottage, and inside the room the toys could see three children lying asleep in a bed. The moon shone on a rag doll that the biggest child was cuddling.

On a table near by was a piece of paper with a beautiful train drawn on it.

'The boy must have done that,' whispered the clown. 'He must be fond of trains.'

The youngest child of all held a very old rabbit in her arms. It had lost one ear and its tail, but it looked very happy because the little girl loved it.

'That's all the toys they've got!' said the clown. 'They look kind children, and I expect they would love us. Shall we climb in at the window and put ourselves on the bed ready for them to see when they wake up?'

Everyone agreed, and one by one the toys climbed in through the window. It was a difficult job hauling the train up with all the carriages, but it was done at last, and soon the moon shone down on a bedful of toys waiting quietly for the daytime.

When the sun shone in through the window, the three children woke up. The boy sat up and yawned. Then he suddenly saw all the dolls, teddy-bears, the clown, soldiers and everything, and he blinked in amazement, thinking he was still asleep.

'Ooh, look!' he cried to his sisters. 'See what's on our bed!'

The little girls woke up and cried out in surprise. One of them picked up a doll and hugged her, and the other cuddled the clown. The boy picked up the clockwork train and looked at it admiringly.

'Mummy, Mummy!' called the children. 'Where did all these toys come from? Did you put them there?'

Their mother came into the room and stared in astonishment at all the toys.

'No,' she said. 'Why, my dears, I couldn't possibly afford to buy you even one of them, and no one would give me so many as that for you!'

'Well, where did they come from, then?' wondered the children. 'Aren't they beautiful? Can we keep them, Mummy? We'll take such care of them.'

'I know you will,' said their mother. 'But what puzzles me is where they came from.'

'Perhaps Santa Claus sent them, and forgot it wasn't Christmas,' said the little girl.

'That must be it!' said the boy. 'Well, we'll look after them well, and won't we be proud of them!'

They kept their word. The toys had never been so well-cared-for or so much loved. They were as happy as the day was long, and never, never wanted to leave the ugly little cottage and go back to the fine playroom they had left.

And what about Diane and David? They were surprised to find nearly all their toys gone when they went into the playroom next morning. They looked for this and they looked for that, but it wasn't any good – the toys were gone.

'Well, it serves you right,' said their mother, sternly. 'You didn't know how to treat your toys, and I expect Santa Claus came along and took them away from you!'

'He didn't!' said Diane, beginning to cry. 'Oh, I wish they hadn't gone. I won't be so horrid again, Mummy, I really won't! Then perhaps the toys will come back.'

But, as you will guess, they never did!

A Puppy
in Wonderland

CHIPS was a round, fat little puppy. He belonged to Alan, James and Kate, and they were all very fond of him. He was rather naughty, because he would chew slippers up, and dig great holes in the garden.

'He's a dear little chap,' said Alan, 'but I do wish he'd stop digging in the garden. Daddy is getting so cross!'

'Let's take him for a walk,' said Kate. 'If we make him tired out, he will go to sleep in his basket, and won't get into any more mischief.'

So they called Chips, and he came bounding up to them, delighted to think that he was going for a walk.

'Where shall we go?' asked Alan.

'Through Heyho Wood,' said James. 'It's such a hot day, and it will be nice and cool there.'

So off they started. It was hot! The sun shone

down, and there was not a cloud in the sky. They were glad to get into the shady wood.

Chips ran here and there, sniffing at the ground in great excitement. He could smell rabbits! Then he saw one! Oh, my goodness, what a to-do there was! He yelped and barked, and tore off as fast as his short legs would let him, tripping and tumbling over blackberry brambles as he went!

'Chips! Chips! Come here, you'll get lost!' cried Alan. But Chips took no notice at all. On he went, bounding through the trees, his little tail wagging like mad. He must catch that rabbit, he really must!

But of course he didn't! The rabbit went diving headlong into its hole, and when Chips came up and looked round there was no bunny to be seen!

'It must have gone into the ground like worms do!' thought the puppy. So he chose a nice green place, and began to dig. He scrabbled the earth with his front paws, and sent it flying out behind him with his back ones. He puffed and panted, snorted and sneezed, and he took no notice at all of the shouts and whistles of the children some distance away.

Suddenly there came a shout of rage. Chips

looked up in surprise, and what did he see but a brownie, dressed in a brown tunic, long stockings and a pointed hat! He was staring at Chips with a very angry look on his face, and the puppy wondered why. He didn't wonder long, because he suddenly remembered the rabbit again, and once more began to dig madly.

That made the brownie crosser than ever. He took a long green whistle from his pocket and blew seven short blasts on it. Immediately a crowd of little men like himself came up.

'Look!' said the first brownie, fiercely. 'Look at that horrid dog! He's dug a hole right in the very middle of the fairy ring which we got ready for the Queen's dance tonight! And he won't stop, either!'

'Stop! Stop, you naughty dog!' cried all the brownies. 'Stop digging at once!'

But Chips took no notice at all. He just went on digging. The brownies didn't know what to do.

'He may bite if we go too near him,' said one. 'But we must catch him and punish him. Why, the Queen won't be able to have her midnight dance tonight!'

'I know how we can get him!' cried a small brownie. 'Let's go and ask the spiders to give

us some of their web! Then we'll throw it round the dog and catch him like that!'

'That's a good idea!' cried all the little men. 'Then we'll take him to prison.'

Chips looked up. He thought the brownies looked very cross indeed. He decided that he would go and find the children. But the brownies had closed round him in a ring, and he could see no way to get through. Then two or three of them came running up with a large net made of sticky spider thread. They suddenly threw it over the puppy – and poor Chips was caught!

He tried to get out of the web, but he couldn't. The brownies dragged him away, and he yelped miserably. The children heard him yelping, and looked at one another.

'Chips is in trouble!' said Kate. 'Quick, come and see what's the matter!'

The three children ran as fast as they could to where they heard the puppy yelping. But when they got there, there was no Chips to be seen. There was only a cross-looking brownie filling in a newly-dug hole.

'Oh!' said the children in surprise, and stopped to look at the funny little man. He looked at them, too, and then went on with his work.

'I suppose you haven't seen our puppy, have you?' asked Kate, at last.

'Oh, so it was your dog, was it?' said the brownie. 'Well, do you know what he has done? Do you see this ring of fine green grass, surrounded by toadstools? It was got ready for a dance tonight, by order of the Queen – and your horrid little dog dug a great big hole in the middle of it. It's all spoilt!'

'Oh dear, I am sorry,' said Alan. 'He really is naughty to do that – but I'm sure he didn't mean any harm. He's only a puppy, you know. He's not four months old yet.'

'Well, he's been taken to prison,' said the brownie. 'He wouldn't even stop when we told him to!'

Kate began to cry. She couldn't bear to think of poor little Chips being taken to prison. Alan put his arm round her.

'Don't worry, Kate,' he said. 'We'll find some way of rescuing him.'

The brownie laughed.

'Oh, no, you won't!' he said. 'We shan't set him free until he's sorry.'

He ran off, and disappeared between the trees. The children stared at one another in dismay.

'We must find Chips!' said Kate. 'Where can they have put him?'

'Look, here are the marks of their footsteps,' said James pointing to where the grass was trodden down. 'Let's follow their tracks as far as we can.'

So they set off. Chips had been carried by the brownies, so they could find no marks of his toes, but they could easily follow the traces left on the long grass by the crowd of brownies.

Through the trees they went, keeping their eyes on the ground. Suddenly the tracks stopped.

'That's funny!' said Alan. 'Where can they all have gone to? Look! They stop quite suddenly just here, in the middle of this little clearing.'

'Perhaps they've flown into the air,' suggested Kate.

'I don't think so,' said Alan. 'That little fellow we met had no wings.'

'Well, did they go down through the ground, then?' wondered James. He looked hard at the grass, and then gave a cry of excitement.

'Look!' he said. 'I do believe there's a trap-door here, with grass growing neatly all over it!'

The children looked down – yes, James was

right. There was a square patch there, which
might well be a trap-door.

Alan knelt down, and after a few minutes he
found out how to lift up the trap-door. James
and Kate looked down the opening in
excitement. They saw a tiny flight of steps
leading into darkness. Alan took out his torch
and flashed it into the hole.

'Look!' he cried, and picked up a white hair.
'Here's one of Chip's hairs. Now we know they
took him down this way! Come on!'

The three children scrambled down. There
were twenty steps, and then a stone platform.
To their great astonishment they saw an
underground river flowing by.

'Well, Chips must have gone this way because
there's no other way for him to go!' said James.
'But how are we to follow! There's no boat to
take us.'

But just at that moment a little blue boat
floated up, and came to the platform, where it
stayed quite still.

'Hurrah!' said Alan. 'Here's just what we
want. Come on, you others.'

They all jumped in at once, and the little boat
floated away down the dark stream. After a

while it came out into the open air, and the children were very glad.

They looked round them in wonder.

'This must be Wonderland!' said Kate. 'Look at all the beautiful castles and palaces!'

'And look at the funny higgledy-piggledy cottages everywhere!' said James.

'And what a crowd of different kinds of fairyfolk!' said Alan. 'Look, brownies, elves, pixies, gnomes, and lots of others!'

'I wonder where the brownies took Chips,' said Kate. 'Shall we ask someone and see if they know?'

'Yes,' said Alan. So they stopped the boat by guiding it gently to the bank, and then asked a passing pixie if he had seen any brownies with a puppy dog.

'Yes,' he said. 'They had him wrapped up in spider's web, and took him to that castle over there.'

He pointed to a castle near by on a steep hill.

'Thank you,' said Alan. Then he turned to the others. 'Come on,' he said. 'We must leave this boat, and make for the castle.'

Out they all jumped, and took the path that led to the castle. It was not long before they were climbing the hill on which the castle stood.

They came to a great gate, and by it hung a bellrope.

Alan pulled it, and at once a jangling noise was heard in the courtyard beyond. The gate swung open, and the children went in, feeling a little bit frightened.

There was no one in the courtyard. Exactly opposite was a door, which stood open. The children went towards it and peeped inside. Just as they got there they heard a sorrowful bark.

'Chips is here!' said Kate, in a whisper. 'Let's go in.'

They crept inside the door, and found themselves in a big hall. At one end was a raised platform on which stood a very grand chair, almost a throne. On it was sitting a very solemn brownie. In front of him, still tied up in the spider's thread, was poor Chips, very much afraid. Round him were scores of little brownies, and they were telling the chief one what he had done.

Kate ran right up to the solemn brownie, and James and Alan followed.

'Please, please let our puppy go!' begged Kate. 'He didn't mean any harm to your fairy ring. He was after a rabbit, that's all.'

'What sort of rabbit?' asked the chief brownie.

'Oh, a big sandy one, with white tips to its ears,' said Alan. 'I saw it just as it ran away from Chips.'

'Then he's a good puppy, not a naughty one!' cried the solemn brownie. 'That rabbit is very bad. It used to draw the Queen's carriage, and what do you think it did?'

'What?' asked the three children.

'Why, one night, it ran away with the carriage and all!' said the brownie. 'The poor Queen was so frightened. The carriage turned over, and she was thrown out. The rabbit ran off, and we have never been able to catch it since.'

'Well, Chips nearly caught it!' said Kate, eagerly. 'And I expect he saw it go into a burrow, and tried to dig it out – only he chose the wrong place, that's all. I'm sure he's very sorry indeed for all the trouble he has caused.'

'Wuff-wuff! Wuff-wuff!' said Chips, sitting on his back legs, and begging for mercy.

'We'll let him go at once!' cried the brownies, and two of them ran to cut away the web that bound him. In a trice Chips was free, and danced delightedly round the three children. Kate picked him up and hugged him.

'Take them back to the wood,' commanded the chief brownie. 'And give Chips a bone to make up for his fright.'

The puppy barked in glee when a large bone was given to him. He picked it up in his mouth and began to chew it.

'The carriage is at the door,' said a little brownie, running in. The children were taken to the great door, and outside in the yard stood a grand carriage of silver and gold, driven by a brownie driver. Six small white horses drew the carriage. How excited the children were!

They all got in, said goodbye to the brownies, and then off went the carriage at a smart pace. It went up hill and down dale, through miles of Wonderland, and at last entered the same wood in which their adventures had started that morning.

'Thank you so much,' said the children, as they jumped out. They patted the horses, and then the carriage turned round and was soon out of sight.

The children walked home, and told their mother all that had happened. But she found it very difficult to believe them.

'Are you sure you haven't made it all up?' she asked.

'Well, look, here is the bone that the brownies gave to Chips!' said Kate. 'And look at his tail! It's still covered with spider's web!'

So it was – and after that their mother had to believe their exciting story, especially as Chips had learnt his lesson, and never, never, never, dug a hole in the garden again!

Snifty's Lamp Post

ONCE upon a time there lived a very disagreeable gnome called Snifty. He was head of the gnome village he lived in, and he was very unkind to everyone.

Now, the Chancellor of Gnomeland came to visit him one night. There was no moon, and it was so dark that the Chancellor could hardly see his way through the village. He drove down the wrong path, and when he got out of his carriage to see where he was, he fell over two or three geese, and then sat down on a frightened pig.

This made him very cross, and when he got to Snifty's house he told him that he ought to be ashamed of having a village which was so dreadfully dark.

'Why don't you have a fine new lamp post put just in front of your house?' he asked. 'Then your visitors would know where you lived, and would not fall over pigs and geese.'

'I will,' said Snifty, rubbing his hands gleefully, glad to think that his villagers would have to buy a fine lamp post for him out of their own money. He didn't once think of buying it himself. He always made his poor people pay for everything, and because they were afraid of him, they did not dare to say no.

So the next day he sent a notice round the village to say that the gnomes were to make him a fine new lamp post. Then when the Chancellor paid him a call another night he wouldn't go the wrong way.

'Will you give us the money for it?' asked the gnomes.

'Certainly not!' answered Snifty. 'What is the use of being the chief if I can't get things for nothing, I should like to know?'

The gnomes knew that it was of no use to say anything more, but they were very angry.

'It's time we made Snifty stop this sort of thing,' they grumbled. 'He's always expecting us to pay for everything, and he never gives us a penny towards it.'

They began to make the lamp post. It was a lovely one, for the gnomes liked making things as beautiful as they could, no matter whether they were working for people they liked or disliked.

Snifty soon sent them word that the

Chancellor was coming to see him again, and he ordered the gnomes to have the lamp post put up in time.

Then the gnomes grumbled even more, and suddenly they decided that they would do just what Snifty said, and no more. They would finish the lamp post and put it up – but they wouldn't put any oil in the lamp, or light it! That would just serve old Snifty right!

So they finished the lamp post and put it up just in front of Snifty's front gate. He watched them from the window, but he didn't bother to come out and say thank you.

The Chancellor arrived that evening, and again it was very, very dark. No one had put any oil in the lamp or lighted it, so there was no light for him to see by again. He was very cross, especially when his carriage got stuck in the ditch and couldn't be moved. He got out, and trod on a hedgehog, which hurt him very much.

'Why doesn't Snifty do as I tell him, and get a lamp post put in front of his gate?' he growled. 'He's rich enough!'

Snifty was very angry when he found that the lamp was not lighted. The Chancellor told him how his carriage had stuck in the ditch, and asked him why it was that he had not got his lamp lighted, to show him the way. Snifty rang a bell, and told his servant to fetch some of the village gnomes, and he would hear why they had disobeyed him.

The gnomes soon came, and Snifty asked them angrily why they had not obeyed him.

'We have obeyed you, Sir,' answered the gnomes. 'You told us to put a lamp post in front of your gate, and we have done so. But you did not tell us to put any oil in it.'

'Oh, you silly, stupid creatures!' cried Snifty, angrily. 'Then hear me now. The Chancellor is coming again tomorrow night, and oil is to be put in the lamp. Do you hear?'

'Yes,' said the gnomes, and went out.

When they had got to their homes they put their heads together and decided that they would again do exactly as Snifty had said – they would put oil in the lamp, but no wick!

So next day oil was poured into the lamp, but no wick was put in. And when the Chancellor arrived that night he again found that he could not see where Snifty lived! This time he jumped out of his carriage too soon, and walked straight into a very muddy pond. He was so angry when he reached Snifty's at last that he could hardly speak.

Once again Snifty called the gnomes to his house, and asked them what they meant by not obeying him.

'Sir, we have obeyed you,' answered the gnomes. 'We have put oil in the lamp as you bade us. You did not tell us to put in a wick – so how could the lamp be lighted?'

'Then put in a wick' shouted Snifty, very angry indeed.

So next day the gnomes put a fine big wick into the lamp, but when evening came, they did not light it.

'Snifty said "put in a wick" – he did not say

light the wick,' said the gnomes grinning among themselves.

This time the Chancellor was so certain that the lamp would be alight that he drove right through the village without seeing it, looking all the time for Snifty's lighted lamp. When he stopped and asked where he was, he found that he had driven three miles beyond the village. So he had to turn his carriage round and go back.

'Are you disobeying me on purpose?' he asked Snifty, when he at last arrived. 'Where is that lamp?'

'Isn't it lighted?' cried Snifty.

'No, it isn't,' answered the Chancellor.

'Then I'll find out why!' cried Snifty in a rage, and he called in the gnomes once more.

'Why have you disobeyed me again?' he shouted angrily.

'We have not disobeyed you!' answered the gnomes in surprise. 'You told us to put a wick in the lamp, and we have done so. We did not hear you order us to light the wick.

'Then tomorrow light the wick!' roared Snifty.

The gnomes consulted among themselves, and decided that the next night they would light the wick as Snifty had commanded, and then blow it out! So they would be obeying him, and yet he still would not have his light.

They did this. One of them lighted the lamp carefully, and then after five minutes he blew the light out. Then they waited for the Chancellor to come as usual.

This time the Chancellor was so angry to find that the lamp was again not lighted for him that he almost deafened Snifty with his shouting. Snifty called in the gnomes again, and they explained that he had told them to light the lamp, and they had done so. He had not told them to let it burn all night long, and as oil was expensive they had blown out the light after five minutes.

Snifty was too furious to speak for a whole minute.

'Tomorrow you will light the wick which rests in the oil, and you will see that the lamp is burning all night long,' he cried at last. 'I will have no misunderstanding this time.'

The gnomes went away. For some time they could not think of any way in which they might again trick Snifty, and yet still obey him. Then one of them had a good idea.

'Snifty didn't say anything about where the

lamp was to be, did he?' he said. 'Let's move it away from his gate when night comes, and put it somewhere else. We'll light it, and keep it burning all night long – but it won't be in the right place!'

The other gnomes thought this was a splendid idea. So when night came, they went quietly to where the lamp post was, and carried it away to the other end of the village, and there they lighted it.

Very soon the Chancellor came by, and seeing the light, he stopped and got out of his carriage. He was very much puzzled when he could see no sign of Snifty's house. He stopped a little gnome and asked him.

'Oh, Snifty lives at the other end of the village,' answered the gnome.

'Oh dear, oh dear!' said the Chancellor. 'What a nuisance! I have got the King of Gnomeland in my carriage tonight, and I didn't want to lose my way as I usually do. I told Snifty to be sure and have the lamp alight outside his front gate, so that I would know where I was.'

Now when the little gnome heard that the King was in the carriage, he was very much surprised. In a trice he had told the other gnomes, and very quickly they lifted up the lamp post and carried it in front of the carriage to show the driver the way. They set the lamp down by Snifty's front gates, and then cheered the King loudly as he drove by.

'What very nice, good-natured fellows,' said the King, pleased. 'Snifty is lucky to have such fine people in his village.'

When they reached the house, the Chancellor told Snifty that again there had been no lamp outside his house, and sternly asked him why. Snifty gasped with rage, and called in his gnomes at once.

'Why have you disobeyed me again?' he cried.

'We haven't disobeyed,' answered the gnomes. 'You told us to light the lamp, and keep it burning all night long. But you didn't say it was to be outside your gates.'

Then Snifty lost his temper, and said some rude and horrid things to the gnomes in front of the King. The King stopped him and asked to be told all the tale. When he found that night after night Snifty had been tricked over the lamp, he was very much puzzled.

'But your villagers seem such good-natured fellows,' he said. 'Why, they carried the lamp all the way in front of my carriage for me! It is very wrong of them to behave like this. After all, it is your lamp, for you have paid for it, Snifty. They have no right to treat it like that.'

'Excuse me, Your Majesty,' said a gnome, stepping forward. 'We had to pay for the lamp, not Snifty. He makes us pay for everything he wants. If he had paid for the lamp himself, we should not have tried to teach him a lesson.'

'Are you poor?' the King asked Snifty.

'No, Your Majesty,' said Snifty, beginning to tremble.

'Then why do you not pay for your lamp yourself?' asked the King. 'Many tales have reached me lately, Snifty, of your meanness, and I came here to find out if they were true or not. I now see very plainly that they are. Your people were quite right to treat you as you deserve. You must leave the village, and I will make someone else the chief!'

So Snifty had to go, and you may be sure nobody missed him. As for the lamp, it now burns brightly outside the new chief's gates every night, and reminds him to be kind and generous. If he isn't, I don't know what trick the gnomes would play on him – but I'm quite sure they would think of something!

The Clockwork Duck

THERE was once a clockwork duck who thought a very great deal of herself. She was made of plastic and floated beautifully. She had a little key in her side, and when she was wound up she paddled herself along in the water.

She lived in the soap dish by the bath, along

with the soap, a sponge, a floating goldfish and a little green frog. When Harry had his bath at night the clockwork duck always swam up and down and made him laugh. Mummy used to wind her up, and when she was paddling herself along, the frog and the goldfish, who could only float, thought she was very wonderful indeed.

'You ought to go out on the pond with the real ducks,' said the frog. 'My, wouldn't they think you marvellous.'

'Yes, you are wasted here,' said the goldfish. 'You should go out into the world.'

The clockwork duck listened, and began to long to go out to the real ducks on the pond.

'They would be so proud to have me with them,' she thought. 'Perhaps they would make me their queen! I am very pretty, and when I am wound up I can swim very fast indeed!'

The more she thought about it, the more she wanted to go. And one day, when Spot the dog came into the bathroom, she called to him and begged him to take her down to the pond in his mouth.

'Very well,' said Spot, in surprise. 'But you'll be sorry you left your nice home in the soap dish, I can tell you! Real ducks haven't any time for clockwork ones!'

He picked up the little duck in his mouth, ran downstairs, went out of the back door, and took the duck to the edge of the pond. He dropped her into the water and left her there.

Soon a large white duck swam up and looked at the clockwork duck.

'What are you?' she said.

'A clockwork duck,' said the duck. 'I am a very wonderful duck. I have a key in my side, and when it is wound up I can swim across the water.'

'Well, I can swim over the pond without being wound up at all!' said the duck. 'I don't think that is very wonderful!'

'You don't know what you are talking about!' said the clockwork duck, crossly. 'You ought to make me queen of the pond, that's what you ought to do! I tell you I am a very marvellous bird!'

By this time other ducks had swum up and were listening to the clockwork duck. Then a frog popped up his green head, and two or three fishes looked out of the water too. The clockwork duck felt that she was making quite a success.

'Wind me up and see how nicely I can swim,' she said.

So the frog swam up to her, took the key in his front fingers and wound her up. Whir-r-r-r, she went, and her legs began to paddle to and fro, sending her quickly over the water.

All the ducks, frogs and fishes laughed to see her, and she was proud to think she had amused them.

'Well, she said at last, 'would you like to make me your queen?'

'You must prove that you are worthy to be a queen first,' said the big white duck. 'Listen – we big ducks want to swim down the pond and get into the little brook, because we have heard that there is plenty of food to be found in the mud there. But we don't want the little yellow ducklings to go with us.'

'Well, I'll look after them for you, and keep them safe,' said the clockwork duck, proudly. 'Just wind me up once more and I shall be all right.'

So they wound her up, and then swam off to the little brook that ran by the end of the pond. The yellow ducklings swam up to look at the clockwork duck who was to look after them, and when they saw that she was no bigger than they were, they laughed.

'Why, you can't be any older than we are,'

they cried. 'We don't want to be looked after by you!'

'You stay with me and be good,' said the clockwork duck, fiercely.

'No,' said the ducklings. 'We want to go after the big ducks and see what food they are finding in the brook. Good-bye!'

With that the naughty little ducklings swam off. The clockwork duck swam after them as fast as she could, but alas! – long before she reached the brook her clockwork ran down, and she could paddle no farther. She could not quack like a real duck, so all she could do was to bob up and down on the ripples, hoping that no harm would come to the yellow ducklings.

Soon she heard a great noise of quacking, and back to the pond came the big ducks with the little ducklings behind them, looking very sorry for themselves.

'What do you mean by letting our ducklings swim off by themselves like that?' quacked the biggest duck, in a temper. 'Do you know that a rat has caught one, and that another got caught in the weeds and couldn't get free!'

'Why didn't you peck them and make them behave?' cried another duck.

'I can't peck,' said the clockwork duck.

71

'Well, why didn't you swim with them and see that no harm came to them?' shouted a third duck.

'I tried to, but my clockwork ran down, and I couldn't swim any farther,' said the clockwork duck, hanging her head.

'Well, you could have at least have quacked loudly, so that we should have known something was happening, and could have come to your help!' said the first duck, fiercely.

'But I can't quack!' said the poor clockwork duck.

'Then what use are you!' cried all the ducks, in a rage. 'You're the stupidest, silliest creature we've ever seen, and as for making you our queen, why, we'd sooner ask that dog over there!'

They swam at the frightened duck, and pecked her so hard that little dents came here and there in her plastic skin. Their quacking disturbed Spot the dog, who was lying asleep in the sunshine. He jumped up and ran to the clockwork duck's rescue.

In a trice he picked her up in his mouth and ran off with her.

'Take me back to my nice home in the soap

dish,' sobbed the poor little duck. 'I don't like the big outside world.'

So Spot ran upstairs and put her gently back into the soap dish with her good friends the goldfish, the sponge and the soap. They were sorry to hear her sad story.

'Never mind, you shall be our queen!' they said. 'But hush! Here comes Harry for his bath!'

Harry trotted into the bathroom, and Mummy ran the water into the bath. She picked up the clockwork duck and wound her up.

'Oh, Mummy!' cried Harry, in surprise. 'Look, how dented and spotted my little duck is! What has done that?'

But Mummy didn't know – and you may be sure that the clockwork duck said never a word!

A Cat
in Fairyland

BIMBO was a big black cat, the finest puss in town. His whiskers were four inches long, his tail was fat and furry. His coat shone like silk, and his purr was so loud that it sounded like a motorbike out in the road!

He belonged to Jenny and Simon, and they loved him very much.

'He is the most beautiful puss I've ever seen,' said Jenny.

'If only he could talk, it would be lovely,' said Simon. 'He's so clever he could teach us a lot.'

Bimbo often used to go out for walks with Jenny and Simon. When they took their tea to Hallo Wood, Bimbo ran behind them, sat down with them, and shared their milk. Then he would go prowling off by himself, not very far away, always keeping the children well in sight.

One day all three started off, their tea in a basket. They went right to the middle of Hallo Wood, sat down and began their tea. When they

had finished Bimbo stalked off on his own, as usual. And suddenly a very strange thing happened.

Jenny happened to look up from the book she was reading and saw a strange little man, rather like a gnome, walking quietly through the trees. On his back he carried a large empty sack. Jenny nudged Simon and both children stared at the gnome in surprise and excitement, for they had never seen any kind of fairy before.

Bimbo didn't see the gnome. He was sitting down, washing himself, purring very loudly. The gnome crept up behind him, opened his large sack, and suddenly flung it right over Bimbo.

Jenny and Simon jumped up at once, shouting angrily. The gnome turned and saw them. At once he pulled the mouth of the bag tight, threw it over his shoulder with poor Bimbo struggling inside, and ran off through the wood. Jenny and Simon followed, fearful and raging, wondering what the gnome wanted with their beautiful cat.

Panting and puffing the gnome tore through the wood, with Jenny and Simon after him. He ran into a thick bush, and when the children came up, he had disappeared. They couldn't see him anywhere.

'Oh, poor Bimbo!' said Jenny, almost crying. 'Where has he been taken to? Oh, Simon, we really must find him and rescue him.'

'Well, I don't see where the gnome has gone to,' said Simon, puzzled. He looked round and ran here and there, but there was no sign of the gnome.

'We'd better go home and tell Mummy,' he said. 'Come on.'

But they had lost their way! They couldn't find the path they had taken in following the gnome, and they were quite lost. Jenny began to feel frightened, and wondered if the gnome would come back and take them prisoner too, but Simon cheered her up, and said that he would fight a dozen gnomes if he could see them.

'There's a little path running along here,' he said to Jenny. 'We'd better follow it. It must lead somewhere.'

So they ran down it, and after some time they came to the prettiest little cottage they had ever seen, so small that it really didn't look much more than a large doll's house. Simon knocked at the yellow front door, and a pixie with silvery wings opened it. She looked so surprised to see them.

'We've lost our way,' said Simon, politely.
'Could you please help us?'

'Come in,' said the pixie. 'Mind your heads.'

They had to stoop down to go inside, for the
door was so small. Inside the cottage were small
chairs and a tiny table. It was the funniest little
place. Jenny was half afraid of sitting down in
case she broke the chair she sat on.

'Let me offer you a cup of tea,' said the pixie,
and she hurried to her small fireplace and took a
boiling kettle off the hob.

'Well, we've really had tea,' said Simon, 'but
it would be nice to have a cup of pixie tea, so
thank you very much, we will.'

Then while the pixie made sweet-smelling tea
in a little flowery teapot, and set out tiny currant
cakes, Simon and Jenny told her all about the
gnome who had stolen Bimbo, their cat.

'Now did you ever hear such a thing!' said
the pixie, in surprise. 'I'm sure I know where
your puss has been taken.'

'Oh where?' asked the children at once.

'To the old wizard, Too-Tall,' said the pixie,
handing the plate of buns to Jenny. 'I know that
his last cat, who used to help him in his spells,
ran away a little while ago, and he has been
wanting another. That gnome you saw is his

79

servant, and I expect he has been looking out for a good black cat. When he saw your Bimbo he captured him at once, and I expect he took him straight to his master, Too-Tall.'

'But Bimbo would hate to help anyone with spells,' said Jenny. 'He's just an ordinary cat, and he would be very unhappy to live away from us. The wizard has no right to take him!'

'Could we rescue him, do you think?' asked Simon. 'Where does this wizard live?'

'He lives in Runaway House, not very far from here,' said the pixie.

'What a funny name!' said the children.

'Well, it's a funny house,' said the pixie. 'It's got four little legs underneath it, and when the wizard wants to move, he just tells it to run where he wants it to, and the legs run away at once, taking the house with them.'

'Goodness me!' said Jenny, her eyes shining with excitement. 'Wouldn't I like to see it!'

'I'll take you there, if you like,' said the pixie, and she wrapped a little coat round her. 'But mind – don't make a noise when we get there, or the old wizard might put a spell on us.'

'Will we be able to rescue Bimbo, do you think?' asked Simon.

'We'll see when we get there,' said the pixie, opening the front door. 'Come along.'

She took them back to the thick bush where the gnome had disappeared. To the children's surprise they saw a little trap-door hidden under the bush. The pixie pulled it open, and all three of them climbed down some steps into an underground passage. Then for some way they walked in darkness, guided only by the pixie's voice in front of them. Soon a little lamp shone out, and Jenny and Simon saw a crowd of little doors in front of them.

The pixie opened a blue one and led the way into a small room, where a grey rabbit was writing at a desk. He looked up, and asked where they wanted to go.

'To Runaway House,' answered the pixie. The rabbit gave them each a green ticket, and told them to sit on three little toadstools in the corner. They all sat down and the rabbit pressed a button. In a trice the three toadstools shot upwards and Jenny and Simon clutched at the edges in surprise.

For a long time they went up and up, and at last the toadstools slowed down. They came to a stop inside another small room, where a second rabbit sat. He took their tickets, opened a door and showed them out into the sunshine.

'What an adventure!' said Simon, who was thoroughly enjoying himself. 'I did like riding on those toadstools!'

They were on a hillside, and the pixie pointed to a little house at the top, surrounded on three sides by trees, to shelter it from the wind.

'That's Runaway House,' she said. 'You can see the feet peeping from underneath it. When it runs it raises itself on its legs and goes off like lightning!'

The three made their way up to it, and the pixie tiptoed to a little window at the back. She peeped inside, and beckoned to the children. They crept up and looked in.

Bimbo was inside! He sat on the floor in the middle of a chalk ring, looking very angry and very miserable. His great tail swept the floor from side to side and his fine whiskers twitched angrily.

The wizard Too-Tall, a thin bent old man in a pointed hat, was standing opposite the cat, waving a long stick. He looked very cross. In a corner by the fireplace was the gnome who had stolen Bimbo, stirring something in a big pot.

'You must help me with my magic spells, or I'

will turn you into a mouse!' said the wizard to Bimbo. And then to the children's enormous surprise, Bimbo opened his mouth and spoke.

'Are your spells all good ones?' he asked. 'For I tell you this, Master Wizard, no cat belonging to my honourable family would ever help in making a bad spell for witches or goblins to use!'

'I am not a good wizard,' said Too-Tall, with a horrid smile. 'I make my money by selling magic to witches, and if you are too grand to help me, my honourable cat, I shall have to do as I said, and turn you into a mouse. Then you will be hunted by your honourable family, and be punished for your stupidity.'

Poor Bimbo began to tremble, but he still would not agree to help Too-Tall, and the wizard grew impatient.

'I will give you one more chance,' he said at last. 'Unless you stand up on your hind legs, turn round twice and mew seven times loudly whilst I chant my magic words and wave my enchanted stick, you shall be changed into a little brown mouse!'

He began to wave his long stick and chant curious words, which made the little pixie outside shiver and shake. But Bimbo did not stand up and mew as he had been told. He sat there in the middle of the ring, looking very much frightened, but quite determined not to help the wicked old wizard.

Then Too-Tall lost his patience. He struck Bimbo with his stick, called out a magic word, and then laughed loudly – for the black cat suddenly vanished, and in its place cowered a tiny brown mouse.

'Now you see what your punishment is!' cried the wizard. 'Go, hide yourself away, miserable creature, and be sure that when I get another cat, you will be hunted for your life!'

The little mouse rushed away into a corner, and hid itself in an old slipper. Jenny and Simon could hardly believe their eyes when they saw that their lovely Bimbo had vanished, and in his place was a poor little mouse. Jenny began to cry, but Simon doubled up his fists, half inclined to go in and fight the wizard and gnome.

'Don't do anything foolish,' whispered the pixie, dragging the two away from the window. 'Hush, Jenny, don't cry, or the wizard will hear you, and he might quite easily change all of us into mice too.'

'But I must do something about poor Bimbo,' said Simon, fiercely.

'Well, I've got a plan,' said the pixie. 'Listen. We'll wait till darkness comes, and then borrow three spades from Tippy, an elf who lives near by. We'll dig a big hole just a little way down the hill. Then we'll all borrow trays and trumpets, and make a fearful noise outside the cottage. The wizard will wake in a fright and think a great army is marching against him. He will order his house to run away, and as the only way it can run is down the hill because there are trees on every other side, it will fall straight into the pit we have dug for it!'

'What then?' asked the children in excitement, thinking it was a marvellous plan.

'Well, I'll pop inside the house before the wizard has got over his fright, and get his enchanted stick,' said the pixie, delightedly. 'He's no good without that, you know. You, Simon, must get hold of the gnome and hold him tightly. You, Jenny, must pick up the little mouse. The wizard will probably run away, for he is an awful coward without his magic stick.'

'Go on, go on!' cried the children, their eyes shining.

'That's all,' said the pixie. 'We'll just run off to Tippy's, then, and I'll see what I can do about Bimbo for you.

A Cat in Fairyland

Night was coming on, for the sun had gone down over the hill. The pixie led the way to a large toadstool on the other side of the hill. It had a little door in it and the pixie knocked. An elf opened the door, and peeped out.

'Who is it?' he asked.

'It's only Tuffy the Pixie,' said the pixie. 'Can you lend us three spades, Tippy?'

'Certainly,' said Tippy, and he took three little spades from a corner of his strange toadstool house. The pixie took them, said thank you, and ran off again with the children. They passed the wizard's house, which was now lighted inside by a swinging lamp, and went a little way down the hillside.

Then they began to dig. How they dug! The pixie said a little spell over their spades to make them work quickly, and the hole soon began to grow. The spades flew in and out, and the children got quite out of breath.

At last it was finished. The moon shone out in the sky, and the pixie said they had better wait for a big cloud to come before they carried out the next part of their plan, for if the house could see before it as it ran, it would run round the hole they had made, instead of into it.

'I'll take the spades back to Tippy's and

borrow a few trays and things,' whispered the pixie. 'You stay here, and watch to see that everything is all right.

It wasn't long before the pixie was back again. She had with her three trays, two trumpets and a large whistle. She giggled as she handed out the things to the children.

'What a shock the wizard will get!' she said. 'Now creep with me just outside the cottage, and when I say 'GO!' bang on your trays and blow your trumpets hard. I'll blow my whistle, and if we don't give the wizard the fright of his life, I shall be surprised!'

They all crept up to the cottage. 'GO!' suddenly shouted the pixie as soon as a cloud came over the moon. In a trice there was a most fearful noise! The trays clanged, the trumpets blared, the whistle blew, and in between all three shouted at the top of their voices.

The wizard was sitting at his table eating his supper with the gnome. When they heard the fearful din outside, the wizard leapt to his feet and turned very pale.

'It's the elfin army after us!' he shouted. 'House, house, find your feet, run away, fast and fleet!'

At once the house stood up on its four legs

and began to move. It raced down the hill, straight towards the big hole that the children and the pixie had dug.

Plonk! It fell right into it. Chimneys flew about, windows smashed, and the wizard and the gnome cried out in terror. They couldn't get out of the door because it was buried in the pit, so they tried to get out of the window.

'Come on!' cried the pixie. 'Into the house, all of you!'

Jenny and Simon rushed to the fallen house. They climbed in at one window, and the pixie climbed in at another. Jenny ran to the corner where she saw the frightened little mouse peeping out of a slipper. She picked it up and slipped it into her pocket.

Simon rushed at the gnome and held him tightly, then called to Jenny to tie him up with a piece of rope he saw lying by the fire. The pixie snatched up the wizard's enchanted stick with a cry of delight.

The old wizard had scrambled out of his window and was rushing down the hill in the moonlight. He was frightened out of his wits!

'Leave the gnome and come away now,' said the pixie. 'If that old wizard meets any witch he knows he may bring her back here, and that would be awkward.'

The three climbed out of the tumbled-down house and ran down the hillside to give back the trays, trumpets and whistle. As they came back again, the pixie pointed to the east with a shout of dismay.

'There's the wizard with two witches! Come on, we shall have to hurry.'

She took the children to the door that led to the toadstool room where the rabbit sat. In a twinkling they had their tickets and were sitting on three toadstools. Just as the strange lifts had started to rush downwards the wizard and witches came racing into the room, and sat down on other toadstools.

'Ooh, my, now we're in for a race!' groaned the pixie. 'Jump off your toadstools as soon as they stop and run for the door. Race down the passage and up the steps to the trap-door as fast as ever you can!'

So as soon as the toadstools stopped, Jenny and Simon leapt off them, ran to the door, and raced into the passage as fast as their legs would take them. The pixie followed, and even as they all reached the door they saw the wizard and witches landing in the room on their toadstools.

They tore along the passage and up the steps, with the wizard and witches after them. When they got outside they banged the trap-door down, but the wizard pushed it open almost at once. Then the pixie gave a shout of triumph.

'What a silly I am! I'd forgotten I'd got Too-Tall's enchanted stick!' she cried. 'I'll soon settle him!'

She waited till Too-Tall and the witches had climbed out of the trap-door, and then she danced towards them, waving her stick and chanting a long string of words.

The wizard gave a howl of fright, and raced back to the trap-door. The witches followed, and soon there was a bang as the trap-door closed.

'They're gone, and they won't come back in a hurry!' said the pixie, in delight. 'What a good thing I remembered I had Too-Tall's stick. I can use it on Bimbo too, and change him back from a mouse to a cat.'

They all hurried to the pixie's cottage. She drew a circle of chalk on the floor, put the frightened mouse in the middle, waved the enchanted stick and cried out a magic word. Immediately the mouse vanished, and in its place appeared Bimbo, the big black cat!

Bimbo gave a loud purr and leapt over to the delighted children. What a fuss he made of them! They stroked him and loved him and he rubbed his big head against them.

'Now what about a hot cup of cocoa and a slice of cake?' asked the pixie. 'It's quite time you went home, you know, or your mother will be very worried about you.'

So they all sat down to hot cocoa and slices of gingercake. Then the pixie showed them the way home through the wood. She shook hands with them, stroked Bimbo and said good-bye.

'Good-bye,' said Jenny and Simon, 'and thank you ever so much for helping us. We only wish we could do something in return for your kindness.'

'Don't forget I've got the wizard's magic stick!' said the little pixie with a laugh. 'I never in all my life expected to have such a wonderful thing as that! That's quite enough reward for me! Now good-bye to you both, and run home quickly.'

Off went Jenny, Simon and Bimbo, and very soon they ran up the path to their house. Mummy was looking for them, and was getting very anxious. When she heard their story she looked most astonished.

'What an extraordinary thing!' she cried. 'I can hardly believe it, my dears.'

'Well, Mummy, we'll get Bimbo to guide us to the pixie's cottage in Hallo Wood tomorrow,' said Jenny. So the next day they told Bimbo to take them there – but wasn't it a pity, he couldn't remember the way!

'Perhaps he will one day,' said Simon. 'We must wait for that.'

And as far as I know, they are still waiting.

The
Very Little Hen

THERE was once a fine fat hen called Chucky,
who laid beautiful brown eggs every single
day. She belonged to Dame See-Saw, and was
one of a big flock, for the old dame made her
living by selling eggs.

Now one day Chucky wandered out of the
old woman's garden. She knew she ought not to
do this, for she had often been warned that the
world outside was not good for hens. But the
gate was open and out she walked.

She hadn't gone very far before she met
Ten-Toes the pixie.

'Good morning,' he said. 'Come here, my
dear, and let me see what sort of an egg you can
lay me for my dinner. I'm very hungry indeed,
and a nice boiled egg would do me a lot of good!'

So Chucky laid him an egg. It was one of her
very best, big and brown, and Ten-Toes was
very pleased. He made himself a fire, put his
little saucepan on to boil, and very soon the egg

was in the bubbling water. Ten-Toes ate it with a crust of bread, and said that it was the nicest he had ever tasted.

'You must come home with me,' he said to Chucky. 'I'd like an egg like that every day.'

'Oh, I can't come with you,' said Chucky, frightened. 'I belong to Dame See-Saw. I must go back.'

'No, no,' said Ten-Toes, and he picked up the fat brown hen. But she struggled so hard, and pecked his finger so badly that he grew angry.

'Ho ho!' he said, in a nasty voice. 'So you think you won't come with me, do you? Well, I'll soon show you that you're wrong.'

With that he tapped Chucky on the head with his wand and said two magic words. In a trice the hen grew much, much smaller – so small that she was no bigger than a buttercup flower!

'Ha!' said Ten-Toes. 'Now you can peck all you like, but you won't be able to hurt me! And when I get you home, I'll change you back to your right size again, and make you lay me an egg every day!'

But when Chucky heard that, she fled off between the blades of grass, clucking loudly in fear. At first she didn't know what had happened to her, but soon she guessed that she had been made very, very small, for the grass towered above her, and the face of a daisy seemed as big as the sun!

She made her way back to Dame See-Saw and told her all that had happened.

But Dame See-Saw was cross. 'What use are you to me now, I'd like to know!' she cried. 'I can't turn you back to your right size again, and all the other hens will peck you. The eggs you lay will be so tiny that I shan't be able to see them. You can just walk out of the garden gate again, and go to seek your living somewhere else!'

Poor Chucky! She ran out of the gate, clucking in despair. Who would have her, now that she was so small?

'I'll go to Tweedle the Gnome,' she thought. 'He isn't very big. Perhaps he'd like to keep me.'

But Tweedle laughed when he saw Chucky.

'What good would your eggs be to me?' he asked. 'Why, I could put twenty in my mouth at once and not know they were there! No, I don't want you, Chucky.'

Then the little hen went to the goblins in the hill, though she was really rather afraid of them. But they didn't like eggs.

'We never eat them,' they said. 'And we couldn't sell them, Chucky, because they are so very tiny. No, we don't want you, Chucky.

Chucky wandered off to the Wise Man, and begged him to keep her, and she would lay him eggs every day.

'But what could I do with them?' asked the Wise Man. 'They're so small that I should have to put on my biggest pair of spectacles to see them. No, Chucky, I don't want you!'

Poor Chucky went away sadly. Nobody wanted her. There wasn't any room for her anywhere. She went on and on until at last she came to a beautiful garden. In one corner of it was built a play-house for the children, and in this they kept all their toys.

There was a rocking-horse, a big shelf full of books, a toy fort, a Noah's ark, two dolls, a toy clown, a teddy-bear, a box of tricks and last of all, a lovely toy farm. The little hen peeped in at the door and thought it was a fine place. She wondered if there was anyone there who would like to have her for their own.

But Peter and Jane, who owned the lovely play-house, were not there. They were staying at their Granny's, so the toys were all alone.

They saw the tiny hen at the door and called to her to come in.

'What a little mite!' they cried. 'Are you alive or are you a toy like us?'

'I'm alive,' said Chucky, and she told the toys her story, and how she could find nowhere to live. Then the toys all began to talk at once, and there was a tremendous noise. At last the teddy-bear held up his hand for silence, and everyone was still.

'Chucky,' said the teddy-bear to the tiny hen, 'would you like to come and live with us here?

98

The Very Little Hen

There is a toy farm over there, with sheep, cows, horses, goats, pigs, ducks and one cock. There used to be a hen, too, but she got broken. The cock that is left is lonely, and as he is just about your size, we are sure he would be delighted to welcome you to his little shed.'

Chucky was so happy that she could hardly speak. She looked at the little toy farm and thought it was the prettiest place she had ever seen. It was all fenced round, and the farm stood in the middle with the barns and sheds here and there. The farmer and his wife, both made of wood, waved to Chucky.

She ran to them, and they bent down and stroked her. She was just the right size for them. Then the little wooden cock strutted up, and admired Chucky. His feathers were only painted on, but Chucky's were real, and he thought she was wonderful.

'Welcome to my shed!' he said, and he led Chucky to the door of a tiny shed near by.

'I think I'll lay the farmer an egg to show how grateful I am,' said Chucky, and she straight-away laid a beautiful brown egg in the little nesting box there. How delighted the farmer and his wife were! All the toys crowded round to see it, too!

'Well, the other hen that got broken never laid an egg in her life!' cried the farmer's wife. 'What a clever little thing you are, to be sure!'

'Let's have some baby chickens!' cried the farmer. 'We won't eat your eggs yet, Chucky. Lay a dozen in the nesting box, and then sit on them. It would be grand to have twelve yellow chicks running about the farm!'

So Chucky laid twelve brown eggs, and sat on them – and do you know, one morning they all hatched out into the tiniest, prettiest yellow chicks you ever saw! Chucky and everyone else were so proud of them! It made the toy farm seem quite real, to have the little chicks running about everywhere.

Tomorrow Peter and Jane are coming back from their Granny's – and whatever will they say when they see the little chicks, each no bigger than a pea, racing about the toy farm, cheeping loudly? I really can't think!

As for Chucky, she has quite forgotten what it was like to be a great big hen. She is happy as the day is long, trotting about with her chicks on the little toy farm.

The Brave
Little Puppy

ONE day, when Martin and Clare were walking home from school, they saw a man throw a little puppy into a pond, and then run off and leave it.

'Oh!' cried Clare in a rage. 'Look, he's tied a brick round the poor little thing's neck, Martin, and he meant to drown it. Quick! Let's get it out!'

Martin took off his shoes and socks, waded into the pond and picked up the struggling puppy. He quickly undid the string that tied the brick round its neck, and then carried the shivering little creature back to the bank.

'Let's take it home, and see if Mummy will let us keep it,' said Clare. 'Poor little thing! What a horrid man that was!'

They carried the puppy home – but, oh dear, Mummy wouldn't let them have it.

'No,' she said, 'you have two rabbits and a kitten and that's quite enough. You can't have a puppy too. Besides, it is a very ugly little thing.'

'But what shall we do with it?' asked Clare.

'Daddy's got to go to town this afternoon and he'll take it to the Dog's Home,' said Mummy. 'It will be looked after there until someone comes and offers to give it a good home. You had better go with Daddy into town, too, and have your hair cut, both of you.'

So that afternoon Daddy and the two children got into a little brown car and drove off to town. Clare carried the puppy, which wriggled and licked her happily, thinking it had found a lovely master and mistress at last. The children thought it was the nicest little puppy they had ever seen, and even Daddy said it wasn't a bad little thing when it had licked the back of his ear a dozen times.

'Here's the hairdresser's,' said Daddy, pulling up by the kerb. 'Come on, you two. Leave the puppy in the car, and we'll all go and have our hair cut.'

So into the shop they went, leaving the puppy in the car. Soon all three were sitting in chairs with big white cloths round them, and snip, snip, snip went the scissors.

Outside the shop were two men. They had

seen Daddy and the children go into the hairdresser's and they knew that it would be some time before they came out again.

'Let's take this car, Bill,' said one of the men. 'We can jump into it and drive off before anyone stops us!'

'But isn't that a dog inside?' said the other man.

'Pooh, that's only a puppy!' said the first man. 'Come on, quick, before a policeman comes!'

He opened the car door, and at the same moment the puppy started barking his very loudest, for he knew quite well that the two men were not the kind children, nor their father. The man cuffed the puppy, and he bared his little white teeth and snarled. He was very much afraid of this nasty rough man, but the car was in his charge, and he was going to guard it as best he could.

So he flew at the man who was trying to sit in the driver's seat, and bit him in the arm with all his might. The man tore him away and flung him into the back of the car, but, still barking, the brave little dog once more hurled himself at the thief.

Then Martin and Clare heard him barking, and Martin ran to the window and looked out.

The Brave Little Puppy

'Daddy, Daddy!' he cried. 'There's two men trying to take the car! Quick! Quick! The puppy is trying to stop them, but they'll soon be away!'

Daddy rushed out of the shop at once, followed by the hairdresser and another man. In a trice they had captured the two thieves and the hairdresser went to telephone the police. In a few minutes the bad men were marched off to the police station, and Daddy and the children went back to have their hair finished.

'Well, that puppy is about the bravest little thing I ever saw!' said Daddy. 'I've a good mind to keep him, after this. He stopped our car from being stolen, there's no doubt of that. What about taking him home again, children, and telling Mummy what he's done? Perhaps she would let you keep him then.'

'Oh, Daddy!' cried Martin and Clare in delight. 'Do let's!'

So they all drove home again with the puppy, and Daddy told Mummy how his bravery had saved their car from being stolen. The puppy looked at Mummy with his brown eyes, and wagged his stumpy tail hopefully.

'Well, we'll keep him!' said Mummy. 'I'm sure he will grow up into a very brave, faithful dog. You shall have him, children.'

The Brave Little Puppy

So that is how Pickles the puppy came to belong to Martin and Clare. He is a grown-up dog now, and twice he has scared away burglars, and once he pulled Baby out of the water when she fell in. Mummy is very glad she let Martin and Clare keep him – and of course they think he is the very best dog in all the world!

The Enchanted Sea

ONE lovely sunny morning John and Lucy went out to play in their garden. It was a very big one, and at the end was a broad field.

'Let's go and play in the field this morning!' said Lucy. So down the garden they ran and opened the gate in the wall, meaning to run out into the green field.

But oh, what a surprise! There was no field there! Instead there was the blue sea – and how Lucy and John stared and stared!

'Lucy! What's happened?' asked John, rubbing his eyes. 'Yesterday our field was here. Today there's a big sea!'

'We must be dreaming,' said Lucy. 'Let's pinch each other, John, and if we each feel the pinch, we'll know we're not dreaming.'

So they each pinched one another hard.

'Ooh!' they both cried. 'Stop! You're hurting!'

'It's not a dream, it's real,' said John, rubbing

his arm. 'But oh, Lucy! It must be magic or something. Let's go and tell Mummy.'

They were just going to run back to the house when Lucy pointed to something on the smooth blue water.

'Look!' she said. 'There's a boat coming – but isn't it a funny one!'

John looked. Yes, sure enough, it was a boat, a very strange one. It had high pointed ends, and at one end was a cat's head in wood and at the other a dog's head. A yellow sail billowed out in the wind.

'Who's in the boat?' said John. 'It looks to me like a brownie or gnome, Lucy.'

'I feel a bit frightened,' said Lucy. 'Let's hide behind our garden wall, John, and peep over the top where the pear tree is.'

They ran behind the wall, climbed the pear tree and then, hidden in its leafy branches, peeped over the top. They saw the boat come nearer and nearer, and at last it reached the shore. Out jumped the brownie, threw a rope round a wooden post near by, and then ran off into the wood to the left of the children's garden.

'Well, that was one of the fairy folk for certain!' said John, in excitement. 'Did you see his pointed hat and shoes and his long beard, Lucy?'

For a long time the children watched, but the little gnome did not come back. After a bit John began to long to see the boat more closely, so he and Lucy climbed down the pear tree and ran quietly over the grass to where the boat lay rocking gently.

'Oh, Lucy, it must be a magic one!' said John. 'Do let's get in it just for a moment to see what it feels like! Think how grand it will be to tell everyone we have sat in a brownie's boat!'

So the two children clambered into the little boat and sat down on the wooden seat in the middle. And then a dreadful thing happened!

The rope round the post suddenly uncoiled itself and slipped into the boat. The wind blew hard and the yellow sail billowed out. The boat rocked from end to end, and off it went over the strange enchanted sea!

'Ooh!' said Lucy, frightened. 'John! What shall we do? The boat's sailing away with us!'

But John could do nothing. The wind blew them steadily over the water, and their garden wall grew smaller and smaller, the farther away they sailed.

'That brownie will be cross to find his boat gone,' said Lucy, almost crying. 'Where do you suppose it's taking us?'

On and on went the little boat, the dog's head pointing forwards and the cat's head backwards. Lucy looked at the back of the dog's head, and thought that it looked a little like their dog at home.

'I do wish we had our dear Rover with us,' she said. 'I'm sure he would be a great help.'

To her great surprise the wooden dog's head pricked up its ears and the head turned round and looked at her.

'If you are fond of dogs, I shall be pleased to help you,' it said.

'You did give us a fright!' said John, almost falling off his seat in surprise. 'Are you magic?'

'Yes, and so is the wooden cat over there,' said the dog. 'We're only wooden figure-heads, but there's plenty of good magic about us. You look nice little children, and if you are fond of animals and kind to them, the cat and I will be very glad to help you.'

'Meeow!' said the cat's head, and it turned round and smiled at the two astonished children.

'Well, first of all, can you tell us about this strange sea?' asked John. 'It's never been here before.'

'Oh yes, it has, but usually at night-time when nobody is about to see it,' said the dog. 'It belongs to the Wizard High-Hat. He sent his servant, the brownie Tick-a-tock, to fetch a red-and-yellow toadstool from the wood near your garden and made the sea stretch from his island to there, so that Tick-a-tock could sail quickly there and back.'

'But I expect he lay down and fell asleep,' said the cat. 'He's always doing that. So when you got into the boat, it sailed off with you instead of the brownie. It doesn't know the difference between you, you see.'

'Oh goodness!' said John, in a fright. 'Does that mean it's taking us to the Wizard High-Hat?'

'Yes,' said the dog, 'and he'll be in a fine temper when he sees you instead of the brownie!'

'Whatever shall we do?' said Lucy, looking anxiously round to see if the wizard's island was anywhere in sight.

'Well, we might be able to help you, if you'll just say a spell over us to make us come properly alive when we get to the island,' said the dog. 'If we were a proper dog and cat we could perhaps protect you.'

'What is the spell?' asked John.

'One of you must stroke my head, and the

other must pat the cat's head,' said the dog, looking quite excited. The cat mewed loudly and blinked her green eyes. 'Then you must say the magic word I'll whisper into your ear, and stamp seven times on the bottom of the boat. Then you'll see what happens when we reach the shore. Don't do any of these things till we reach the island.'

The dog whispered the magic word into each child's ear, and they repeated it again and again to themselves to make sure they had it right. Then suddenly Lucy pointed in front of the boat.

'Look!' she said. 'There's the island – and, oh my! Is that the wizard's palace on that hill in the middle?'

'Yes,' said the dog. 'You'll see some of his soldiers in a minute. They always meet the boat.'

Sure enough the children saw six little soldiers come marching out of the palace gates towards the shore. They were dressed in red, and looked very like John's wooden soldiers at home.

The boat sailed nearer and nearer to the shore, and the dog told John and Lucy to use the spell he had taught them. So John stroked the dog's head, Lucy patted the cat's head, and each of

them said the magic word, and then stamped
loudly on the bottom of the boat seven times.

And what a surprise they had! Each wooden
head grew legs and a body, and hey presto, a
live cat and dog jumped down from the ends
of the boat and frisked round the children in
delight!

'We're real, we're real!' they cried. 'Now we
can go with you and help you.'

The boat grounded on the sandy shore and
the rope flew out and tied itself round a post.
The chief of the soldiers stepped up and looked
most astonished to see the two children.

'Where's Tick-a-tock the brownie?' he asked,
sternly. 'What are you doing here?'

'Well, you see, we stepped into the brownie's
boat and it sailed off with us,' said John. 'We're
very sorry, and please would you ask the wizard
to excuse us and send the boat back to our
garden to take us home again?'

'You must come and ask him yourself,' said
the soldier. 'You are very naughty children!'

The six soldiers surrounded John and Lucy
and marched them off towards the palace on the
hill. The dog and cat followed behind, and the
soldiers took no notice of them.

Soon the children were mounting the long

flight of steps up to the castle, and were pushed into a large hall, where sat the Wizard High-Hat on a silver throne. He looked most surprised when he saw John and Lucy, and at once demanded to know how they got there.

John told him, and he frowned.

'Now that is most annoying,' he said crossly. 'I want to send my sea to another place tomorrow, and that means that Tick-a-tock won't get back with the toadstool. I shall keep you prisoner here for a hundred years, unless you can do the things I tell you to do.'

Lucy began to cry, and John turned pale.

'Please don't set us very hard tasks,' he said. 'I'm only eight years old, and Lucy's only seven, and doesn't know her six times table yet.'

The wizard laughed scornfully, and commanded his soldiers to take the children to the bead-room. They were led to a small room with a tiny window set high up. On the floor were thousands and thousands of beads of all colours and sizes.

'Now,' said the wizard, 'your first task is to sort out all these beads into their different colours and sizes. You can have today and tonight to do this in, and if you haven't finished by tomorrow morning you shall be my prisoners for a hundred years.'

With that he closed the door with a bang, and he and his soldiers tramped away. The children looked at one another in dismay.

'We can never do that!' said Lucy, in despair. 'Why, it would take us weeks to sort out all these beads!'

'Where are the cat and dog?' asked John, looking all round. 'They don't seem to be here. They might have helped us.'

Suddenly the door opened again, and the dog and cat were flung into the room, panting. Then the door closed again, and the four were prisoners.

'We thought we wouldn't be able to get to you!' said the dog. 'So I bit a soldier on the leg and the cat scratched another on the hand, and they were so angry that they threw us in here with you!'

'Just see what we've got to do!' said Lucy, in despair, and she pointed to the beads. 'We've got to sort out all these before tomorrow morning.'

'My word!' said the dog, blowing out his whiskered cheeks. 'That's a dreadful job! Come, Puss! Let's all set to work.'

The Enchanted Sea

The four began to sort out the beads, and for an hour they worked steadily. Then the door opened and a soldier put a loaf of bread, a bone, a jug of water and a saucer of milk into the room. Then the door shut and the key was turned.

The children ate the bread and drank the water. The dog gnawed the bone and the cat drank the milk.

'It's no use going on with these beads,' said the cat, suddenly. 'We shall never get them done. I know what I'll do!'

'What?' asked the children, excitedly.

'You wait and see!' said the cat, and she finished her milk. Then she washed herself. After that she went round the little room, and looked very hard at every hole in the wall.

'Now watch!' she said. She sat down in the middle of the floor and began to make a curious squeaking noise that sounded like a thousand mice squealing at once – and a very curious thing happened!

Out of the mouse holes round the room there came running hundreds of little brown mice. They scampered to where the cat sat, and made ring after ring round her. When about a

117

thousand mice were there, the cat stopped
making the curious noise and glared at the mice.

'I could eat you all!' she said, in a frightening
voice. 'But if you will do something for me, I
will set you free!'

She pointed to the beads. 'Sort those out into
their different colours and sizes!' she said. 'And
be quick about it!'

At once the thousand mice scuttled to the
beads. Each mouse chose a bead of a certain
colour and size and carefully put it to start a
pile. Soon the little piles grew and grew, and
the big pile sank to nothing. In half an hour all
the thousands of beads were neatly sorted out
into hundreds of piles of beads, all of different
colours and sizes.

'Good!' said the cat to the trembling mice.
'You may go!'

Off scampered the mice to their holes and
disappeared. The children hugged the clever
cat, and thanked her.

'Now we'll let the wizard know his task is
done!' said the cat. 'Kick the door, John.'

John kicked the door and an angry soldier
opened it.

'Tell the wizard we've finished our work,'
said John, and the soldier gaped in astonishment

to see the neat piles of beads. He fetched the wizard, who could hardly believe his eyes.

'Take them to the Long Field!' said High-Hat to his soldiers. So the children, followed by the cat and dog, were taken to a great field which was surrounded on all sides by high fences. The grass in this field was very long, almost up to the children's knees.

'Here is a pair of scissors for each of you,' said the wizard, with a cunning smile. 'Cut this grass for me before morning, or I will keep you prisoner for a hundred years!'

The children looked at the scissors in dismay. They were very small, and the grass was so long and there was such a lot of it! The wizard and his soldiers shut the gate of the field and left the four alone together.

'Well, I don't know what we're going to do this time!' said John, beginning to cut the grass with his scissors, 'but it seems to me we're beaten!'

He and Lucy cut away for about an hour, but at the end of that time their hands were so tired, and they had cut so small a patch of grass that they knew it was of no use going on. They would never even get a tenth of the field cut by the morning.

'Can't you think of something clever to help us again?' asked John at last, turning to the cat and dog.

'We're both thinking hard,' said the cat. 'I believe the dog has an idea. Don't disturb him for a minute.'

The dog was lying down, frowning. Lucy and John kept very quiet. Suddenly the dog jumped up and ran to Lucy.

'Feel round my collar,' he said to her. 'You'll find a little wooden whistle there.'

Lucy soon found the whistle, and the dog put it into his mouth. Then he began to whistle very softly. The sound was like the wind in the grass, the drone of bees and the tinkling of faraway water.

Suddenly, holes appeared in the earth all around the high fence, and hundreds of grey rabbits peeped out of them. They had dug their way into the field under the fence, and as soon as they saw the dog blowing on his magic whistle, they ran up to him and sat down in rings round him. He took the whistle from his mouth and looked at them.

'I chase rabbits!' he said. 'But I will let you go free if you will do something for me. Do you see this beautiful green juicy grass? Eat it as

121

quickly as you can, and you shall go the way you came.'

At once the rabbits set to work nibbling the green grass. It was very delicious and they enjoyed it. In an hour's time the whole field was as smooth as velvet, and not a blade of grass was longer than Lucy's little finger.

'Good!' said the dog to the rabbits. 'You may go!'

At once they scampered away. John ran to the gate in the fence and hammered on it. The wizard himself opened it, and when he saw the smooth field, with all the long grass gone, he gasped in astonishment.

'Where's the grass you cut?' he asked at last, looking here and there.

The children didn't know what to say, so they didn't answer. The wizard grew angry, and called his soldiers.

'Take them to the top most room of my palace and lock them in!' he roared. 'They have been using magic! Well, they'll find themselves somewhere they can't use magic now!'

In half a minute the soldiers surrounded the children and animals again and hustled them back to the palace. Up hundreds and hundreds of stairs they took them, and at last, right at the very top, they came to a room that was locked. The wizard took a key from his girdle and unlocked the door. The children and animals were pushed inside and the door was locked on the outside.

By this time it was almost night-time. A tiny lamp burnt high up in the ceiling. There was one window, but it was barred across. John looked round in despair.

'Well, I don't see what we can do now!' he said, with a sigh. 'I'm afraid, cat and dog, that even you, clever though you are, can't do anything to help us.'

The dog and cat prowled all round the room, but the walls were strong and thick, and the door was locked fast. For a long time the four sat on the floor together, then suddenly the cat jumped up and ran to the window.

'Open it!' she said. 'I want to see if I can squeeze through the bars.'

Lucy and John opened the heavy window, and the cat jumped lightly on to the ledge.

'What's the good of squeezing through the bars?' asked John, peering down. 'You could never jump down, Puss! Why, we're right at the very top of the palace!'

The cat squeezed through the bars and stood

on the outer window ledge. Her green eyes shone in the darkness.

'There's another window ledge near by!' she whispered. 'I will jump on to that, and see if the window there is open. If it is, I'll go in, and see if I can find some ways of helping you all to escape!'

With that she jumped neatly to the next window ledge, and disappeared. The window there was open and the brave cat leapt lightly into the room. The palace was in darkness. Wizard, soldiers and servants were all sleeping. The soft-footed cat ran down the stairs, and at last reached a room from which loud snores came. She ran in, and by the light of a small candle saw the wizard asleep on his bed. On the table near the candle lay his keys!

In a trice the cat had them in her mouth and back she went up the stairs, leapt on to the window ledge, and then jumped on to the next ledge, mewing to the children as she jumped. How excited they were to see the keys!

John fitted them one by one into the lock of the door until he found the right one. He turned it, and the door opened! Quietly the two children, the cat and the dog slipped down the hundreds of stairs and undid the heavy palace door. Out they went into the moonlight, and ran down to the seashore.

'I do hope the sea still stretches to our garden wall,' said John. 'Hurry up, little boat, and take us home again.'

The boat set off over the water. Suddenly Lucy gave a cry and pointed to each end of the boat. The dog and cat had disappeared, and once more the two wooden figure-heads stood high at each end.

'The magic is gone from them!' said Lucy. 'Oh, I do hope they don't mind. They're gone back to wooden heads again.'

'Don't worry about us,' said the dog. 'We've enjoyed our adventure, and we're quite happy. I only hope the boat will take you home again.'

On and on sailed the little ship in the bright moonlight. After a long time John caught Lucy's arm and pointed.

'Our garden wall!' he said, in delight.

'Who's that on the edge of the sea?' asked Lucy, seeing a little figure standing there.

'It must be Tick-a-tock the brownie!' said John. 'How pleased he will be to see his boat coming back again. I expect he thought he was quite lost.'

The boat touched the grass, and the children

jumped out. They called good-bye to the dog and cat, and then felt themselves pushed aside. The brownie had rushed up to his boat, and leapt in as quickly as he could. The sails filled out and off went the boat in the moonlight, the dog barking and the cat mewing in farewell.

'That's the end of a most exciting adventure,' said John. 'Goodness, I wonder what Mummy has been thinking all this time! We'll tell her all about our adventure, and in the morning perhaps Daddy will make us a raft and we can all go exploring on the magic sea.'

Mummy was glad to see them. She had been so worried. She could hardly believe her ears when she heard all that had happened.

'You must go to bed now,' she said. 'But tomorrow we'll all go down to see the enchanted water, and perhaps Daddy will sail off to the wizard's island to punish him for keeping you prisoner.'

But in the morning the sea was gone! Not a single sign of it was left – there were only green fields and hills stretching far away into the distance. The wizard had called his sea back again, and although John and Lucy have watched for it to return every single day, it never has. Isn't it a pity?

The Goldfish
that Grew

HOPPETTY had a goldfish in a glass bowl, the prettiest little thing you could wish to see, and the pixie was very proud of it indeed. But what puzzled him was that it didn't grow! It kept as small as could be, and Hoppetty became quite worried about it.

'I give it plenty of good food,' he said, 'and it has a nice piece of green water-weed in the globe, and a little black water-snail for company. I do wonder why it doesn't grow.'

But nobody could tell him why.

'Perhaps it isn't very happy,' said Mrs Biscuit, the baker's wife. 'I've heard it said that unhappy creatures never grow much.'

Hoppetty couldn't bear to think that.

'I'm very kind to it,' he thought. 'It ought to be happy. How dreadful if people should think it doesn't grow because I'm unkind to it and make it unhappy!'

He gave the fish more food than ever, but it

wouldn't eat it. The water-snail feasted on it instead, and that made Hoppetty cross. He really didn't know what to do!

Then one day, as he walked over Bumble-Bee Common, he saw a pointed hat sticking up among the gorse bushes, and he knew a witch was somewhere near by. Hoppetty peeped to see.

Yes, sure enough a witch was there, sitting on the ground beside a little fire she had made. On it she had placed a kettle, which was boiling merrily. Soon she took it off, and held over the flames a little fish she had caught in the river near by. She meant to have it for her dinner.

The fish was very small and the witch was hungry.

'I could eat a much bigger fish than you!' Hoppetty heard her say to the little dead trout. 'I think I'll make you bigger, and then I shall have a fine meal!'

She laid the fish down on the grass, and waved her hand over it twice. 'Little fish, bigger grow, I shall like you better so!' she chanted, and then said a very magic word that made Hoppetty shiver and shake, it was so full of enchantment. But goodness! How he stared to see what happened next! The little fish began to grow and grow, and presently the witch took it up and held it once more over the flames, smiling to see what a fine meal she had!

A great idea came to Hoppetty. He would run straight home, and say the spell over his little goldfish! Then it really would grow, and everyone would be so surprised.

Off went Hoppetty, never stopping to think that it was wrong to peep and pry and use someone else's spell when they did not know he had heard it. He didn't stop running till he got home, and then he went straight to his little goldfish swimming about in its globe.

He waved his hand over it twice. 'Little fish, bigger grow, I shall like you better so!' he chanted, and then he said the very magic word, though it made him shiver and shake to do so.

All at once the goldfish gave a little leap in the water, and began to grow! How it grew! Hoppetty couldn't believe his eyes! It was soon twice as big as before, and still it went on growing!

'You're big enough now, little fish,' said Hoppetty. 'You can stop growing.'

But the fish didn't! It went on and on getting bigger and bigger, and soon it was too big for the bowl.

'Oh dear!' said Hoppetty in dismay. 'This is very awkward. I'd better fetch my washing-up bowl and put you in that.'

He popped the fish in his washing-up bowl, but still it went on growing, and Hoppetty had to put it into his bath.

'Please, please stop!' he begged the fish. 'You're far too big, really!'

But the fish went on growing, and soon it was too big for the bath. Then Hoppetty really didn't know what to do.

'I'd better take my fish under my arm and go and find that old witch!' he said at last. 'She can tell me how to stop my goldfish from getting any bigger. Oh dear, I do hope she won't be cross!'

He picked the goldfish up, and wrapped a wet handkerchief round its head so that it wouldn't die, and set off to Bumble-Bee Common. How heavy the fish was! And it kept getting heavier and heavier too, because it went on growing. Hoppetty staggered along the road with it, and everyone stared at him in surprise. Then a gnome policeman tapped him on the arm.

'You are being cruel to that fish,' he said. 'He is panting for breath, poor thing. Put him in that pond over there at once.'

Sure enough the wet handkerchief had slipped off the fish's head, and it was opening and shutting its mouth in despair. It wriggled and struggled, and Hoppetty could hardly hold it. He went to the pond and popped it in. It slid into the water, flicked its great tail and sent a wave right over Hoppetty's feet.

Then who should come by but that witch! Hoppetty ran to her and told her all that had happened, begging her to forgive him for using her spell.

'Do you mean to say that you were peeping and prying on me?' said the witch in a rage. 'Well it just serves you right, you nasty little pixie! Your fish can go on growing till it's bigger than the town itself, and that will be a fine punishment for you!'

'Madam, tell the spell that will make the fish go back to its right size,' said the policeman, sternly. 'Hoppetty has done wrong, but you cannot refuse his request now that he has asked your pardon.'

The witch had to obey. She went to the pond and waved her hand over it twice. 'Big fish, smaller grow, I shall like you better so!' she chanted, and then she said another magic word. At once the great goldfish shrank smaller and smaller, and at last it was its own size again. Hoppetty cried out in delight, and ran to get a net to catch it.

But that little fish wouldn't be caught! It wasn't going to go back into a tiny glass globe again now that it had a whole pond to swim about in, and frogs and stickle-backs, snails and beetles to talk to. Oh no!

Hoppetty had to give it up and he went sadly back home.

'I've lost my little fish,' he said, 'but it serves

me right for peeping and prying. I shan't do that again!'

And I don't believe he ever did!

The Goblin
in the Train

ALL the toys in the playroom were most excited. Tomorrow the clockwork train was going to take them to a pixie party, and what fun that would be.

But, oh dear, wasn't it a shame, when Andrew was playing with the train that day, he overwound it and broke the spring. Then it wouldn't go, and all the toys crowded round it that night, wondering what they would do the next night when they wanted to go to the party.

'I'm very, very sorry,' said the clockwork train. 'But I simply can't move a wheel, you know. My spring is quite broken. You won't be able to go to the pixie party, because I can't take you. It's all Andrew's fault.'

'Well, he must have broken your spring by accident,' said the rag doll. 'He's very careful with us, generally. But it is dreadfully disappointing.'

'Couldn't we send a message to the little

135

goblin who lives under the holly bush?' said the teddy-bear. 'He is very clever at mending things, and he might be able to mend the broken spring.'

'Good idea!' cried the toys, and they at once sent a message to the goblin. He came in five minutes, and shook his head when he saw the broken spring.

'This will take me a long time to mend,' he said. 'I doubt if I'll get it done by cock-crow.'

'Please, please try!' cried the toys. So he set to work. He had all sorts of weird tools, not a bit like ours, and he worked away as hard as ever he could. And suddenly, just as he had almost finished, a cock crew! That meant that all toys and fairy folk must scuttle away to their own places again, but the little goblin couldn't bear to leave his job unfinished.

'I'll just pop into the cab of the train,' he called to the toys. 'I'll make myself look like a little driver, and as Andrew knows the spring is broken, perhaps he won't look at the train today or notice me. Then I can quickly finish my work tonight and you'll be able to go to the party!'

The toys raced off to their cupboard, thinking how very kind the goblin was. He hopped into the cab, sat down there, and kept quite still, just as if he were a little boy driver.

Andrew didn't once look at his engine that day, and the toys were so glad. When night came again the goblin set to work, and very soon he had finished mending the spring. He wound up the engine, and hey presto, its wheels went round and it raced madly round the playroom.

'Good! Good!' cried the toys. 'Now we can go to the party! Hurrah! What can we do to return your kindness, goblin?'

'Well,' said the goblin, turning rather red, 'there is one thing I'd like. You know, I'm rather an ugly little chap, and I've never been asked to a pixie party in my life. I suppose you wouldn't take me with you? If you could, I'd drive the train, and see that nothing went wrong with it.'

'Of course, of course!' shouted the toys in glee. 'You shall come with us goblin, and we'll tell all the pixies how nice you are!'

Then they all got onto the train, the goblin wound it up again, and they went to the party. What a glorious time they had, and what a hero the goblin was when the toys had finished telling everyone how he had mended the broken train!

He drove them all safely back again to the

playroom and then, dear me, he was so happy and so tired that he fell fast asleep sitting in the cab!

And in the morning Andrew found him there and was so surprised.

'Look, Mummy, look!' he shouted. 'The train has suddenly got a driver, and goodness me, the spring is mended too! Isn't that a strange thing! And isn't he a nice little driver, Mummy? Wherever could he have come from?'

But Mummy couldn't think how he could have got there.

'He must have been there all the time and you didn't notice him before,' she said.

'No, Mummy, really,' said Andrew. 'I've often wished my clockwork train had a driver, and I know I should have noticed him if he had been here before. Oh, I do hope he stays. He looks so nice and real.'

The goblin was so happy to find that Andrew liked him and was pleased with him. But he was happier still that night when all the toys crowded round him and begged him to stay and be one of them.

'We like you very much,' they said. 'Don't go back to your holly bush, but stay here and be the driver of Andrew's train. We'll have such fun together every night!'

The goblin wanted nothing better than to stay where he was, for he had often been very lonely under his holly bush.

'I'd love to stay!' he said. 'Come on, I'll take you for a fine ride round and round the playroom!' The toys almost woke Andrew up with their shouts of delight.

Andrew is very proud of his train-driver. He shows him to everyone, and I do hope you'll see him for yourself some day. Then perhaps you can tell Andrew the story of how he got there.

Other great reads from **Red Fox**

Further Red Fox titles that you might enjoy reading are listed on the following pages. They are available in bookshops or they can be ordered directly from us.

If you would like to order books, please send this form and the money due to:

ARROW BOOKS, BOOKSERVICE BY POST, PO BOX 29, DOUGLAS, ISLE OF MAN, BRITISH ISLES. Please enclose a cheque or postal order made out to Arrow Books Ltd for the amount due, plus 22p per book for postage and packing, both for orders within the UK and for overseas orders.

NAME _____

ADDRESS _____

_____

Please print clearly.

Whilst every effort is made to keep prices low, it is sometimes necessary to increase cover prices at short notice. If you are ordering books by post, to save delay it is advisable to phone to confirm the correct price. The number to ring is THE SALES DEPARTMENT 071 (if outside London) 973 9700.

Other great reads *from* **Red Fox**

Two Enid Blyton books in one!

MR TWIDDLE STORIES

Mr Twiddle is a silly but lovable old man. He's always losing things—like his hat and his specs—he has trouble with a cat, gets bitten by a goose and, no matter how he tries, he just can't remember anything! This collection contains two complete books in one!

ISBN 0 09 965560 8   £1.99

MR PINKWHISTLE STORIES

Mr Pinkwhistle is small and round with pointed ears and bright green eyes. And he can do all sorts of magic . . . This collection gives you two complete books about Mr Pinkwhistle in one!

ISBN 0 09 954200 5   £1.99

MR MEDDLE STORIES

Mr Meddle is a naughty little pixie who simply *can't* mind his own business. He always tries to help others but by the time he's fed birdseed to the goldfish, sat in the butter, gone to bed in the wrong house and chased a policeman, people usually wish they'd never set eyes on him. This collection of stories gives you two complete books about Mr Meddle in one!

ISBN 0 09 965550 0   £1.99

Other great reads from **Red Fox**

Adventure Stories from Enid Blyton

THE ADVENTUROUS FOUR

A trip in a Scottish fishing boat turns into the adventure of a
lifetime for Mary and Jill, their brother Tom and their friend
Andy, when they are wrecked off a deserted island and stumble
across an amazing secret. A thrilling adventure for readers from
eight to twelve.

ISBN 0 09 9477009   £2.50

THE ADVENTUROUS FOUR AGAIN

'I don't expect we'll have any adventures *this* time,' says Tom,
as he and sisters Mary and Jill arrive for another holiday. But
Tom couldn't be more mistaken, for when the children sail along
the coast to explore the Cliff of Birds with Andy the fisher boy,
they discover much more than they bargained for . . .

ISBN 0 09 9477106   £2.50

COME TO THE CIRCUS

When Fenella's Aunt Jane decides to get married and live in
Canada, Fenella is rather upset. And when she finds out that
she is to be packed off to live with her aunt and uncle at Mr
Crack's circus, she is horrified. How will she ever feel at home
there when she is so scared of animals?

ISBN 0 09 937590 7   £1.75

School stories from Enid Blyton

THE NAUGHTIEST GIRL IN THE SCHOOL

'Mummy, if you send me away to school, I shall be so naughty there, they'll have to send me back home again,' said Elizabeth. And when her parents won't be budged, Elizabeth sets out to do just that—she stirs up trouble all around her and gets the name of the bold bad schoolgirl. She's sure she's longing to go home—but to her surprise there are some things she hadn't reckoned with. Like making friends . . .

ISBN 0 09 945500 5 £1.99

THE NAUGHTIEST GIRL IS A MONITOR

'Oh dear, I wish I wasn't a monitor! I wish I could go to a monitor for help! I can't even think what I ought to do!'

When Elizabeth Allen is chosen to be a monitor in her third term at Whyteleafe School, she tries to do her best. But somehow things go wrong and soon she is in just as much trouble as she was in her first term, when she was the naughtiest girl in the school!

ISBN 0 09 945490 4 £1.99